MAKING A BETTER WORLD

MAKING A BETTER WORLD

MICHAEL LACOY

Monteverdi Press

ISBN: 978-0-9600689-5-1 (hardcover)
ISBN: 978-0-9600689-3-7 (paperback)
ISBN: 978-0-9600689-4-4 (ebook)
LCCN: 2020922535

Monteverdi Press
Concord, New Hampshire
www.monteverdipress.com

Cover illustration by Lupe Galván
Cover design by Dissect Designs

Typesetting services by BOOKOW.COM

Happy is the man who finds wisdom.

Proverbs 3:13

ONE

"Wait—Grammy Perilloux is going to live with us?"

"Mm-hmm," Oscar said, munching on a bite of toast. "Though it's just temporary ... Hopefully." This last was muttered to himself, but the child caught it and her little brows scrunched.

Her name was Gabriella, though Oscar and everyone else called her Gabby—very appropriately, as it turned out. The kid loved to talk. She said, "Doesn't she have her own house?"

"No."

"Why?"

"Not everyone has their own house. A lot of people don't."

The child's brows re-scrunched. "Where does she live again?"

"Hanover. Come on now—eat. We're going to be late."

The child put a spoonful of raisin bran into her mouth and started chomping. "Why doesn't she like Hanover anymore?"

Oscar paused. On principle he was opposed to lying, and to falsity and deceit of any sort. He was a plain-talker, a straight-shooter, especially with his little girl. But he wasn't about to tell the kid that her grandmother had been kicked out of a retirement home for disciplinary reasons. The Wickham Hill Assisted Living administrator that Oscar had spoken to mentioned multiple and repeated infractions involving drinking, smoking, abusive language, physical threats against other residents, and—what proved to be the final straw—a charge of running a crooked poker game. No, Oscar felt, the child didn't need to hear about any of *that*. When she was older, sure; but not now. He said, "Sometimes people like to move. You know, see new places. It's fun."

Gabby considered this, then nodded, approvingly. She took another bite of cereal. "Where's she going to sleep? In the living room?"

"No. My room."

"Your room?"

"Yep."

"Where are you going to sleep?"

"In my studio."

"Upstairs?"

"Yes." By trade, Oscar was a painter. He made landscapes in oil—vibrant, colorful pictures of forests and rivers and plant life. He was represented by a gallery in Boston, and every now and then sold things directly to collectors. Despite this, however, he had yet to make any significant money from his art, and over the past few years he had begun to find it difficult to meet his bills. To help with expenses he would take on the occasional portrait commission—and painted both people and pets.

"How long is she staying?" Gabby said.

"I don't know. As long as it takes to find her a new place to live. Come on, eat."

Chomping another bite, the child said, "Does she have a dog?"

"No."

"Does she have a cat?"

"No."

"Does she have a hamster?"

"No, she does not have a hamster. In fact, I hate to tell you, bunny, but she's not crazy about animals." Oscar was thinking back to his own childhood, when "Grammy Perilloux"—aka Stella Perilloux—had repeatedly refused to let him have a dog or even a parakeet. Of the latter she had said, "I'm not gonna listen to some damn parakeet squawking all day. You wanna see some birds, go take a walk in the woods."

Gabby was staring at him, aghast. Animals were her obsession, and she had already declared to Oscar and her teachers at the Lizzy Poppins Elementary School that she was going to work in a zoo someday, or be like Jane Goodall and live in the jungle with monkeys. The kid loved monkeys. Though last year her favorite animal had been dolphins, and she had wanted to be like Jacques Cousteau. She said, "What about Mindy? She won't be mean to her will she?" Mindy was their small but excitable dog, a two-year-old mutt whose greatest joys in life were barking at strangers and chewing up Oscar's furniture when he was away from the house. The dog was now out in the backyard, chewing up sticks and rubber doggie toys.

"No, no," Oscar said gently. "She'll be nice to Mindy ... Probably."

"What about Pippy and Tippy?" Pippy and Tippy were the girl's goldfish.

"Pippy and Tippy will be fine. Now finish up. We're leaving in ten minutes."

* * *

"All set?" Oscar said over the loud engine.

From under her helmet and yellow-tinted ski goggles, both of which Oscar had picked up at a local yard sale, Gabby energetically nodded and flashed her excited smile, revealing a missing lower tooth.

Dressed in her minor league softball uniform, which consisted of white pants and an orange T-shirt that read "Vinny's Lube and Oil Change," the child was safely ensconced in the sidecar of Oscar's 1965 Triumph motorcycle. He had bought the bike on eBay in the months following Lila's death, a sort of desperate impulse buy. Something to distract him from his grief. The thing had been in terrible shape—ripped seat, busted brake cables, missing speedometer and tachometer, and a non-working engine, among other issues. Yet over the next two years Oscar rebuilt the bike and added the sidecar for his little girl. He'd finished the project the previous fall, and to their great amusement father and daughter had gone on a number of rides before the weather turned cold, including a couple of times to school where crowds of curious kids gathered around for a closer look.

Now, late May, the bike was back on the road for the new season. Oscar eased out the clutch, moseyed down the dirt driveway, looked both ways for oncoming traffic, then roared off onto Pleasant Street. It was a warm sunny day, mid-70s, no humidity—perfect for a ride and a softball game. With few cars on the road they sped past houses with flowering trees and blooming shrubs, then past Beauville High School and after that past Beauville Hospital. Soon the trees grew denser and the houses more scarce. Oscar turned onto a road with old farms and rolling fields.

With the wind pressing against him, and the motor rumbling beneath him, he gave the bike's horn two quick beeps. Gabby looked up at him and he pointed off to the right. In the low sky about a hundred feet away a bald eagle was gliding alongside them above the green pasture. The hooked yellow beak, the white-feathered head, and the powerful brown body were clearly visible, and for some time the large bird kept up the pace. At first he was just soaring, but then he began flapping his wings as though determined to keep up with the bike. Five, ten seconds later the bird abruptly veered toward the road, soared over Oscar and Gabby, and reversed direction. Oscar glanced at his daughter and saw she was in rapture.

* * *

With the motorcycle's tires turning up a great cloud of dust, Oscar pulled into the ballpark, zipped down a dirt drive past a row of parked cars, and brought the bike to a halt near the third-base bleachers. Carried by its own momentum, the dust cloud continued forward and engulfed father and daughter, then slowly dispersed. A handful of little girls, who'd been standing near the field with their parents, ran up to meet them. The kids were jubilant, some in orange "Vinny's Lube and Oil Change" T-shirts, others in light-blue "Lucky Garden Restaurant" T-shirts. With the youngsters waving and calling out greetings Oscar revved the roaring engine and elicited many happy cheers. He then killed the engine and was immediately besieged by requests from several of the girls asking if they could have a ride.

"After the game," he told them, hoping that by then these seven and eight year olds would have forgotten.

Gabby undid her seatbelt, removed her helmet and goggles, put on her orange "Vinny's" cap, then climbed out of the sidecar with her mitt.

"Have fun out there," Oscar said, giving her a smile.

"I will!" the child said, and she ran off with the rest of the girls.

Dismounting the bike, Oscar started toward the bleachers and saw his brother Duncan, standing with another parent near the third-base dugout. Both Duncan and the parent—a guy named Sy Dubek, a bigwig at Beauville Savings Bank—were watching Oscar, and neither of them looked too impressed. In fact, Duncan looked downright irritated, his eyes cold and staring, his lips twisting sourly. Oscar wasn't surprised. His brother was an irascible guy, thin-skinned and hot-tempered, and always had been.

Turning to Duncan, Sy respectfully, even deferentially, shook his hand before slipping off toward the first-base bleachers.

"Something you said?" Oscar quipped, addressing his brother as he glanced over at Sy Dubek's receding figure.

Duncan scowled. "When are you going to grow up? You make a spectacle of yourself and the kid, driving around like a Hells Angel. Forty-five going on eighteen."

"Calm down," Oscar said calmly. "Gabby loves the bike."

"Yeah, now she does, but that's because she's not class conscious yet. In a couple years she'll be embarrassed—by you *and* the bike. Believe me." With a sneer, Duncan then took in Oscar's getup: black Chuck Taylors, skinny jeans, black T-shirt. "And I see you dressed for the occasion. You look like you're still in high school for God's sake."

"And what do you look like?" Oscar said, taking in Duncan's getup: shiny brown penny loafers, pressed chinos, and a pink oxford button-down. "A proctologist? Seriously, who wears penny loafers to his kid's softball game?"

Fire came into Duncan's eyes. "A grownup, that's who! A mature adult. Unlike you Oscar, I have a reputation in this town. People know me. They expect certain standards."

"You got that right," Oscar said. "And if they don't know you, all they have to do is look out to center field."

At this, the two brothers turned to the ball field. In dead center, above the fence and between two flagpoles—one flying the American flag, the other the New Hampshire state flag—was a large sign. It featured a full-color picture of Duncan's face, at least six feet high. Like a seasoned politician, he displays his large white teeth in a relaxed, winning grin, projecting an air of dependability and trust. And to the left of his face were the words,

PERILLOUX FIELD

A gift to the City of Beauville from Perilloux Motors

"Come on by!"

"Come on by!" was Duncan's signature slogan, which he used in newspaper ads and television commercials to promote his Perilloux Motors empire of four local dealerships.

"And you think *my* kid's going to be embarrassed in a couple years?" Oscar said.

The color came into Duncan's cheeks. "Always the wiseass," he spluttered, becoming enraged but trying not to make a scene. "For years I've put up with this!"

Alas, it was true. Oscar couldn't deny it. From childhood on the brothers Perilloux had been at each other's throats, and it was easy to see why. They had been competitive but unequally blessed. Duncan was better looking, but Oscar was taller. Oscar was smarter, but Duncan tried harder. Duncan was responsible and followed the rules, Oscar was irreverent and did as he pleased. Duncan was the better student, but Oscar the better athlete. The teachers loved Duncan, but the cheerleaders loved Oscar. Duncan worked his ass off to get a 1400 on the SATs, Oscar rarely cracked a book but got a 1600. Duncan went to UMass, Oscar went to UPenn. Duncan got an MBA, Oscar got an MFA. Oscar loved art, Duncan loved money. Now, Duncan owned a successful business, while Oscar lived check to check. Duncan was rich, Oscar was poor.

In short, each of them had plenty of ammo with which to attack the other. Because Duncan had two years on Oscar, and had been physically stronger, he had always gotten the better of their childhood fisticuffs. As kids he had given Oscar more than a few bloody noses. In response, Oscar had opted for another tactic. If he couldn't best his brother with punches, then he would do so with words. By age ten he had mastered the art of the stinging fraternal putdown, and from adolescence on he had loved nothing more than to make withering cracks about Duncan's appearance, his music, his girlfriends, his clothes.

At the same time, and due to their rough upbringing, it had been Duncan who had helped to raise Oscar. When they were still children their father died and their mother started drinking and staying out late, often leaving the kids to fend for themselves.

It was Duncan who made sure he and Oscar were fed, had clean clothes, and went to school.

Remembering all of this now, as he often did after insulting his brother, Oscar felt the sting of guilt. "I'm sorry," he said, and he meant it.

But Duncan wasn't in a forgiving mood. He scoffed, shook his head, and fell into a bitter silence, focusing on the field of play. Coach Cusamano of Vinny's Lube and Oil Change was hitting groundballs to his infield—including to Duncan's daughter Bonnie. Gabby was out in left field, playing catch with another girl who kept throwing the ball over Gabby's head.

At last Oscar said, "So how are things?" His tone was peaceable, conversational.

Not taking his eyes from the field, Duncan shrugged, his expression still disgruntled. "Busy," he said.

Oscar nodded, and waited for more. But more didn't come. Still nodding, he said, "Me? I'm good. Thanks."

Again Duncan shook his head, but now with a half-smile. His tense face relaxed a smidge. "What's going on with Ma? Have you heard anything?"

"Yeah. She's moving in with me. This week—"

"*What?* Are you crazy?"

Oscar raised a helpless hand, as if to say "What are you going to do?"

"Hey, you know what? It's none of my business," Duncan said, now peeved. "You do what you want to do, and have fun. Just don't come running to me when it goes to shit, OK?"

"Look, I know you have strong feelings about this, but there are other places where she could stay."

"Right. Other places so long as I pay for them."

"Duncan, come on. You've got plenty of money—"

"Hey, screw you! For ten, fifteen years I carried her. When you were down in New York playing the starving artist, I was up here bailing her out left and right. *Me*. Not you, not Willie, not Sarah—just me." Willie and Sarah were Stella's two eldest children from her first marriage. Both now lived on the West Coast, and neither had been in touch with Stella for years. "And after her operation, it was me who paid for the treatments, and me who got her into that chichi retirement home. Ten grand a month, and not a penny from any of you. Not one penny!"

"I didn't have it," Oscar said.

"And was she even grateful?" Duncan went on. "Did she ever say 'Thank you Duncan'? Did she ever call to see how I was doing or even my kids? No, she only called when she needed money, and believe me, there was always something. Some excuse, some scam—somebody owed her money; the IRS was after her; she'd cashed some bad checks and the cops were going to arrest her. I'm telling you, the woman's a grifter, and I want nothing to do with her. And believe me, she's going to con you too. No good will come of this."

"Duncan, she has no money. And nowhere else to go."

"Well she should have thought about that before they kicked her out. You know, they didn't even want her at Wickham Hill. When I drove her up there to drop her off, the director came out to meet her and immediately she insults the guy. Made a crack about his wig, something about Liberace. And suddenly the guy starts talking about a waiting list. I couldn't believe it!

I said, 'What are you talking about?' On the phone he told me he had several places. But now he starts giving me this bullshit about 'unexpected contingencies' and 'first come, first serve' and all sorts of other crap, and in the end I paid him off. Another ten grand! And so what does she do? I mean, here she is, living in by far the nicest place of her life—they've got an indoor pool, a movie theater, two restaurants—and she starts running a fixed poker game! She was marking the cards, Oscar! I'm telling you the woman is trouble, and she always has been. Always. She ruined my childhood!"

Oscar sighed. "Hey, that may be true—"

"It sure as hell is true! All of it!"

"OK. But we can't just let her live on the street. I told her she could stay with me till we find another arrangement. A nursing home she can afford. Also, I'm told she's not doing well, with the emphysema. If you could help pay for a place, it might only be for a few years. I could pitch in … a couple hundred a month."

"Oh that's generous. A couple hundred a month from you, and a couple thousand from me."

"Duncan, you're the millionaire. And many times over, if I had to guess."

"No. I refuse. And knowing her, she'd live to a hundred and twenty just to bleed me dry. I'm telling you, I want nothing to do with her. Give Willie and Sarah a call, tell them it's time they stepped up."

"I did. They're not interested."

"See? There you go. You do what you want Oscar, but I'm done."

"OK," Oscar said, and he let it go. The conversation was over.

Out on the field, the warm-ups continued. Oscar was about to suggest they take their seats in the bleachers when a voice came from behind. It was a woman's voice, saying, "Hi Duncan."

Oscar turned—and his heart stopped. Standing before him, in person, was Ms. X.

TWO

Ms. X—Oscar's unwanted obsession.

He had first seen her, and had only *ever* seen her, at church: Sacred Heart of Mary, in Beauville. It began just after Christmas, five months earlier. Since then Ms. X had become a regular parishioner. Sunday after Sunday she would appear with her identical twin daughters, who were roughly Gabby's age, and not once had she come with a man. Together, the three of them would always sit in the same spot: several rows ahead of where Oscar and Gabby always sat, and on the opposite side of the center aisle. At first Oscar hadn't given Ms. X much notice; she was just another congregant in an otherwise sparsely attended church. But as the weeks passed, one after the other, she began to attract more and more of his attention. Very discreetly, his eye would drift across the aisle, mid-Mass, and he would observe the woman—her face, her figure, her clothes, her unadorned ring finger. He would observe as well the way she conducted herself and how she interacted with those around her, and especially how she interacted with her children. Typically the girls would flank their mother, one on each side, and every now and then Ms. X would rest a hand on each of the girls' outer shoulders, enveloping them in a gentle embrace. Holding their missalettes, the girls would run an index finger across the page, as though following the words as the priest spoke them. Doing this, the girls would sometimes look up questioningly at their mother, and Ms. X would lean over and whisper to them, as if to explain a concept or define a difficult word. At first Oscar had thought this merely cute. But over time he had come to find it moving, maybe even deeply moving: a mother's love in action, tender and giving, a selfless response to the children's dependence and unthinking trust. Witnessing the closeness of this young family had touched Oscar, had stirred something in his heart. All in all, he found Ms. X very agreeable. At the same time her very existence was unsettling. Disturbing, even. Her emotional hold on him—completely unsought, and unwanted—had been growing by the week, like some adolescent infatuation, some high school crush. It was absurd! He was a middle-aged widower, not some horny teenager looking for a date! The gold wedding band was still on his finger, and at no time before had he even considered taking it off.

Yet late at night, alone in his bed, when Gabby was snoozing away and no doubt dreaming of monkeys or dolphins or hamsters, Oscar found himself struggling with thoughts of Ms. X.

* * *

"*Oh*—hello," Ms. X said, her face and voice perking up with recognition.

Stupefied by this miraculous appearance, Oscar was speechless. Mouth agape, he just stared. Duncan, who was entirely unstupefied, stepped closer to her and said, almost apologetically,

"This is my little brother … *Oscar*." The name was said tersely, as though it was something of an embarrassment.

"I think we go to the same church," Ms. X continued, addressing Oscar in a patient, helpful tone, as though he might be someone of limited intelligence. "Sacred Heart?"

"Oh … sure," he finally said. "Yeah, I thought you looked familiar."

At the woman's side were her two little ones, each wearing a "Lucky Garden" uniform and cap. They also wore matching glasses, and had dark brown hair cut the same length, down past their shoulders.

Extending a hand to Oscar, Ms. X said, "Margot Saadeh."

Like one in a dream Oscar said, "*Margot* … I like that." For months he had wondered about her name, and now he had learned it—*Margot*. Yes, he liked it. Very much. He also had wondered what she looked like up close, face-to-face. Her eyes, he noticed, were beautiful: warm, intelligent, and very dark.

"You can let go of her hand, Oscar," Duncan said.

Margot chortled, innocently amused, and Oscar released her.

Convinced he had said something witty, and evidently pleased as well that it had come at Oscar's expense, Duncan assumed a triumphant air. With a gloating grin he stepped in front of Oscar, showing him his back, and turned to Margot. "We should sit down," he said to her in a confidential tone.

"Mom, we have to go!" piped up one of the girls.

"We're really late!" said the other one.

"Of course," Margot said. "You guys go on. I'll be here in the bleachers."

"But *these* are the Vinny's Lube and Oil Change seats," said the first one, to which the second one added, "The Lucky Garden seats are over *there*." She pointed to the first-base bleachers.

"That's OK," Margot said, "they're all the same. I'm going to sit with Duncan."

A look of horror came over Oscar's face, his dream turning into a nightmare. Ms. X wants to sit with … *Duncan?*

"OK," the girls said, and scampered off.

"Aren't they lovely," Duncan said in a honeyed voice, watching the girls run around the backstop to the opposite dugout. Then to Margot he repeated, in the same honeyed voice, "Let's sit."

She looked at Oscar. "Are you joining us?"

Duncan glared at Oscar, his eyes savage and fierce. And just perceptibly he shook his head—"*No!*"

"Sure," Oscar said. "Why not?"

* * *

Surrounded by a smattering of parents in hats and sunglasses, the three of them sat in the fourth row of the bleachers, with Margot in the middle. She turned first to Oscar. "It's great to finally meet another parent from church. I'm surprised at how few young families go there. It's mostly just older people."

"Yeah, well … a pedophile scandal will do that."

"*No!*" Margot said, cringing. "Are you serious?"

"I'm afraid so. It happened about ten years ago, before I got here."

"My God," she said. "It's so disgusting. And tragic. The priest is gone, I hope?"

"He's in prison."

"Good ... Those poor kids. And their families. How many were involved? Was it just boys?"

"Yes. Just boys. And quite a few from what I heard."

Margot shook her head, dismayed.

"Maybe we should talk about something else," Duncan said. He gave Oscar the eye as if to say, "Why don't you beat it?"

Margot said, "Hey, did you guys see that motorcycle in the parking lot? The one with the passenger car?"

Duncan frowned.

"Yeah. It's mine," Oscar said.

"Oh, that's so cool!" Margot said. "My girls loved it. Where did you get it?"

Oscar told her and she said, "And you rebuilt it yourself?"

"Yes."

"That's really great. I love stuff like that. I always wanted to renovate an old house. Do it myself. I think it would be very satisfying ... But the motorcycle—I bet it's fun to ride in."

Oscar's brow went up. "Yes," he said, looking at her. "It *is* fun to ride in."

At this, Duncan intervened. Apparently he had heard enough. "You know what?" he said, leaning forward from the bench and looking first at Oscar, and then at Margot. "I'm thinking it might be better if I sat in the middle. I haven't seen my brother in a while, and this way I could talk to both of you." He gave her his relaxed, winning grin, the grin he used in his Perilloux Motors TV commercials and newspaper ads, and now on his billboards in softball fields.

"Oh of course," Margot said, helpful as could be.

She slid down the bench and Duncan took her place beside Oscar. Crossing his arms and surveying the field from this new vantage, Duncan seemed pleased. "Yeah, this is better," he said.

"Hold on," Margot said, leaning forward to look past Duncan to see Oscar. "You said you're new here?"

"I grew up here. But I went to college in Philadelphia, then I moved to New York. I was there for almost twenty years. I went to art school there too."

"Wow," Margot said, breaking into a smile. "I just came from New York, the kids and I. Back in December. And so where did you live?"

"A few places. But the last ten years were in Greenpoint."

"OK," she said, nodding, "I can see that. You've got that Brooklyn look. A bohemian."

"Former bohemian," Oscar said. "Now I'm a dad who goes to church."

Margot laughed, delighted. Duncan was less amused, his expression perturbed, his nostrils flaring.

"And what art school?" Margot said.

Oscar told her.

"Yes, I know it," she said. "For a couple of years I lived near Washington Square Park. I went to some exhibitions there. So you're an abstract painter?"

"I was."

"You stopped?"

"No. I paint landscapes now."

"Traditional landscapes?"

"More or less."

"That's a switch."

"It was," Oscar said, smiling as he recalled the reaction of friends and critics who'd thought his transition to landscapes a very retrograde move.

"And why did you do that?"

He shrugged. "Basically, I got sick of wasting paint."

Margot laughed, though with puzzled eyes. "What does that mean?"

Grinning along, Oscar said, "It means I stopped believing in what I was doing. It was derivative, and boring. Bad de Kooning. And then one day, when I was looking at a tree in Central Park —it was a huge old beech, with these amazing maroon leaves— it hit me that nature was more beautiful than anything I could invent."

"And that was good?"

"Extremely. It was very liberating. Just like that I realized I was surrounded by potential subjects. Everywhere I looked there was something interesting to paint."

Margot was smiling, taking this in. "And that's what you do for a living?"

"Yes."

"That's fantastic. I really love painting. I used to go to the Met quite a bit. It's one of my favorite places in New York."

"It's one of my favorite places too," Oscar said, thrilled.

Duncan rolled his eyes. Then, to no one in particular, he said, "The game's starting."

Onto the field ran the Lucky Garden starting nine.

"Go Lucky Garden!" Margot shouted. "Woo-hoo!"

* * *

This was Vinny's Lube and Oil Change's second game of the season, and Gabby's first year of softball. At last week's home opener the child had struck out and popped to the catcher, and in the fourth inning she had sat down in the grass out in left field, looking bored. From the bleachers Oscar had called out to her, telling her to stand up.

On her first at-bat today the child whiffed on three straight pitches, and when she swung on the third strike her helmet slipped down over her face, covering her eyes and causing her to stumble in sightless confusion. This drew some muffled laughs from the fans. And as Gabby headed back to the bench, Duncan murmured to Margot, "That's Oscar's girl."

Yet when Bonnie came to bat, Duncan gushed with enthusiasm. "Come on babe! Give it a ride!"

Bonnie was Duncan's youngest child, from his second marriage. The first marriage had produced Morgan (a girl) and Skyler (a boy), both now in their late teens. The kids' mother, an estate lawyer, had taken the children and a good chunk of Duncan's money back to her Connecticut hometown. Duncan's second wife, a former model and stage actress, had run off with one of Duncan's salesmen and left Bonnie with her father. This was three years ago. To raise the child Duncan had hired what proved to be a series of temporary nannies. Apparently none stayed more than a few months.

With her first swing Bonnie sent a grounder to third base. Amid many cheers—Duncan himself had leapt to his feet, shouting "Run, Bonnie, run!"—the third-base girl scooped up the ball and promptly threw it over the head of the first-base girl. Reaching the base, Bonnie came to a halt and beamed with deep pleasure. But then—as she gradually understood that the play was not over, that many excited voices were telling her to keep running—she took off for second. The second-base girl moved over to cover the bag, but Bonnie plowed into her and knocked her to the ground. The throw from the first-base girl, with no one now in position to catch it, sailed into left field. Bonnie straightened her helmet, assessed the situation, then took off for third, where she came to a stop just before the ball was thrown back to the infield.

Clapping furiously, Duncan was ecstatic. "Way to go, babe! *Way to go!*"

Still seated, Oscar was doing his best to suppress a grin. Very casually he said, "Duncan … *Duncan.*" He grabbed his brother by the forearm.

"What?" Duncan said, annoyed.

Oscar pointed to second base. The little girl that Bonnie had knocked over still lay on the ground. She was crying and surrounded by her coach and teammates. The umpire was also coming out to have a look, though as he was walking and not running it appeared the injury was likely not too serious. As for the little girl—it was one of Margot's twins.

"Oh shit," Duncan muttered. He sat down and said, to Margot, "Hey, I'm sorry. I didn't even see that. I don't know what happened."

With a severe look Margot was focused not on Duncan but on the drama at second base. "It's all right," she said, keeping her eye on her daughter. "But Bonnie was very rough. It wasn't necessary. She threw an elbow—I saw it."

Now shamefaced, Duncan made no reply.

But in the end the girl was fine. She wiped the tears from her eyes, pouted for a bit, then put her hat back on and took up her mitt. The game went on.

* * *

That night Oscar was back in a dreamy state. He was sitting on the sofa with Gabby, who was now dressed in her PJs. For about the tenth time that year they were watching *The Wild Stallion*, Gabby's current favorite movie. Each of them was also working on a bowl of pistachio ice cream. Every Saturday night father and daughter did this—a movie and a treat. Tonight, though, Oscar wasn't following the exploits of the film's two young heroines, Hanna and CJ. By now he knew the story and even most of the dialogue by heart. Instead Oscar was mentally reviewing his day, recalling his time spent with Margot Saadeh.

Over the past few months, as he had speculated about Ms. X, imagining who she might be and what she might be like, Oscar had known full well that he was playing a fool's game. In his mind the fantasy Ms. X was bright, witty, cultured, and, of course, single and looking to meet someone—someone like him, for instance. But the realist in Oscar, the Oscar who had seen forty-five years of life, the Oscar who had experienced his fair share of disappointment and loss, knew that the actual Ms. X might prove something very different. In reality she might be, oh, you know—shallow, or crazy, or tetchy, or vain. Or any number of unpleasant things. She might even be married, despite the lack of a ring. Part of him was prepared for this. And another part of him was even hoping it might be so, hoping that Ms. X might prove a disappointment or be unavailable in some way. Because then he would be free of this growing obsession, and thus free of the sense that he was betraying Lila.

But no. Oscar's fears had been groundless. The real-life Ms. X, the flesh-and-blood Margot Saadeh, had proved neither shallow, nor crazy, nor tetchy, nor vain, nor even married. Not once but twice over their ballpark conversation she had used the phrase "my ex." In addition to painting and the Met, she had spoken of her interest in cooking and travel, and about her former job at a Manhattan think tank focused on homelessness. She said she had moved to New Hampshire to be closer to her sister, who lived in the nearby town of Scruton. The sister taught at a private day school that Margot's girls attended.

Of course, Oscar thought now, as he ate another spoonful of ice cream, he had only spent a few hours with her. There was much yet to see and learn, much yet to discover about Margot Saadeh. But still—what a first impression! Without question he wanted more. And more he would get.

After the final out was called at the softball game, and all the parents were saying their goodbyes before departing with their kids, Margot had flashed Oscar a warm smile and said, "I guess I'll see you at church."

THREE

The next morning Oscar felt a bit nervy. A bit tense. He was be-hind the wheel of his fifteen-year-old Sorolla sedan, his thoughts focused solely, and comprehensively, on Margot Saadeh.

For her part, Gabby was still worked up over last night's movie. Strapped into the front passenger seat, and barely able to see over the dashboard, the child said, "Daddy, when I grow up, I want to have a ranch just like the ranch on *The Wild Stallion*."

Though Oscar's eyes were focused on the road, his mind's eye was filled with a vision of Margot's warm smiling face. He kept remembering her from yesterday: her curious sociable manner, her dark pretty eyes, the way she had laughed at several of his attempted witticisms. To his daughter Oscar said, "Mm-hm."

Encouraged, the child continued: "And I want to have horses and wild stallions, but also a special place for monkeys. Not cages but a big open place in the woods for them to live and so I can go visit them, and bring them bananas. And also, I want to teach the smart monkeys how to ride the horses, because I think that would be cool, and also funny ..." The child giggled, and looked at Oscar.

They were less than a minute from Sacred Heart. Less than a minute from *her*. Distractedly Oscar said, "Yep ... funny."

"And also," Gabby went on, "I want to have an area for ponies, so little kids can come over after school and go for a pony ride. And maybe this year I can get a pony too, for my birthday …"

They were now a block away from the church, and with some alarm Oscar realized that his body was in a state: his palms sweating, his heart thumping fast.

"Daddy?"

"Yes, I heard," Oscar muttered, keeping his eye on the road. "Your birthday … a pony." What madness this was, he thought —what nonsense! He really was acting like a kid, like a lovesick teenager. It was ridiculous, absurd! With fiery resolve he determined not to pay any attention at all to Margot Saadeh this morning. Instead his attention would be focused exclusively where it should be—on the priest, on the Mass, on God.

* * *

Yet when Oscar entered the church, his eye instantly rebelled. His hungry searching gaze spotted Margot in her usual place, flanked as usual by her little girls. Oscar and Gabby walked up the center aisle, genuflected, and took *their* usual place. They knelt, prayed—or, in Oscar's case, attempted to pray, as Margot's presence made it difficult for him to concentrate—and stood once the organ kicked in.

Holding up the processional cross, a tall pole topped by a gold crucifix, the adult altar server entered the nave from a side door near the front. Next came the reader carrying the Book of the Gospels, and finally the priest, Father Butler, dressed in green vestments. As the procession made its way down the side aisle, around the back, and up the center aisle, the handful of faithful belted out "Lift High the Cross."

Missalette in hand, and pretending to sing along, Oscar peeked across the aisle. From this angle he could see the back of Margot's head and part of her profile. For purposes of discreet observation, he was perfectly positioned. For several seconds he watched as she sang, taking in her thick dark hair, the maroon sweater that clung to her torso and arms, the gray trousers that outlined the form of her—

And just then, life surprised Oscar. Margot's head swiveled around, owl-like, and she looked right at him.

Oscar went stiff, rigid as steel pipe. He tried not to cringe, but he could feel his cheeks burning. Indisputably, she had caught him checking her out. No ifs, ands, or buts about it.

But Margot didn't seem to mind. Just the opposite. She gave him a smile, the same genial smile she had given him several times the day before.

*　*　*

After Mass, Oscar and Gabby waited for Margot and the girls outside the church. When the Saadehs appeared, Gabby said "Hi" and waved at the twins, even though they stood just four feet away. The twins likewise said "Hi" and they both waved back. Introductions were made—the girls were named Zora and Sana —and yesterday's softball game was briefly discussed. Everyone agreed it was fun. Margot then asked Oscar if he was going to the coffee social, over in the church hall. Oscar had never been to the coffee social. And quite frankly, he had never even considered going to the coffee social. But he promptly said "Yep."

Inside the hall they were greeted by a handful of smiling seniors. One of them, a seventyish guy and a Sacred Heart regular, gave Oscar a sly grin and a conspiratorial wink, as if to suggest he was onto him. He knew what Oscar was up to, the old guy seemed to say. Oscar ignored the wink and asked Margot if he could get her a coffee. She said yes and he filled two paper cups, and warned her it was hot. Gabby and the twins had already wandered over to the food table, laden with donuts, Danishes, juice, and fruit.

Now alone with Margot, Oscar kicked off the conversation. "So how was your night? Did you do anything fun?" It was meant as a joke, as he was thinking that she too had probably watched a movie with her offspring. If not *The Wild Stallion*, then perhaps *The Adventures of Bailey the Lost Puppy*, or some other such masterpiece.

"The night was … OK," Margot said uncertainly, mulling the question. "We went to Chez Henri."

"Oh—that's a great place," Oscar said, surprised. Chez Henri was the most expensive restaurant in Beauville, though it seemed an odd choice for a single mom and her two kids. Oscar glanced over at the girls. The three of them remained by the food table, chattering away while munching on doughy treats.

"Yeah, I'd never been. But it was good," Margot said. "It was Duncan's choice."

"*Duncan?*" Oscar said.

"Yes."

"Duncan … *Perilloux?*"

Margot laughed, as though she thought he was joking. But then her expression became puzzled, as though she now thought he *wasn't* joking. "Yes," she repeated.

Stunned by his own blindness, by his failure to see what he should have seen or at least suspected yesterday at the softball game, Oscar flushed mightily. Even his ears felt hot. Sure, he had known that Margot had wanted to sit with Duncan, but he'd thought it was just a friendly thing, that they knew each other from softball, or from … somewhere. Certainly not that there was anything romantic going on! But how was it possible? How could it be? Ms. X … *with Duncan?* Now Oscar felt stupid, and foolish. He fell silent and the conversation stalled.

Finally Margot said, "And how was your night?"

"*My* night? … It was … It was great," Oscar said. "Yeah, a good time." As if to emphasize this point he began coolly nodding his head while taking in the room. The old guy who had winked at him was still watching, and now he gave Oscar a surreptitious thumbs-up: *Go get 'em tiger!* Oscar grimaced, drank his coffee, and scalded his tongue. "Ow, ow … God!"

"Are you OK?" Margot said.

"Yeah … I'm fine. Burnt my tongue."

There was another silence, and this one felt strained.

At last Margot said, "And what about your wife? Is *she* Catholic?"

"*My wife?*" Oscar said, now looking even more pained.

Margot appeared confused. "Yes," she said, and as if to clarify, she glanced purposefully at the gold wedding band on Oscar's left hand, the hand that was gripping his coffee cup.

Now wishing he was anywhere but here, Oscar said, "My wife's ... dead ... She died."

"Oh ... I'm so sorry. I didn't know. Duncan never mentioned it."

"It was about three years ago."

There was sympathy in Margot's eyes; a look of pity. But slowly, her expression changed. It became more meditative, more thoughtful, as if she was maybe pondering the implications of a guy still wearing his wedding band three years after the fact.

Holding half-eaten donuts, the three girls came up to their respective parent. Gabby stood at Oscar's side, and Zora and Sana flanked their mother, assuming what seemed their natural positions. Grateful for the distraction, and hoping to reverse what was fast turning into a morning from hell, Oscar smiled at the twins. He couldn't tell them apart, but the odds were fifty-fifty, so he picked one and said, very cheerily, "How are you Zora?"

The girl's brow darkened. "I'm *Sana*," she said.

"Oh."

"*I'm* Zora," the other girl said, her brow also darkening.

"Right," Oscar said.

Then, as if taken aback, Margot gasped: "*Oh my.*" She was gazing down at Gabby.

"What?" Oscar said, concerned.

Not taking her eyes off the child, Margot said, "Sweetie ... who cuts your hair?"

Very proudly Gabby beamed, showing Margot her missing lower tooth: "Daddy!"

Margot stared at Oscar, and though he could see she was fighting it, there was something like horror in her eyes.

Wanting nothing more than to turn and crawl away, exit the church hall on hands and knees, Oscar shrugged and said, "Her mother used to cut her hair. Now I do it."

Still beaming, Gabby added, "And Daddy cuts his own hair too—and sometimes I help!"

Everyone looked up at Oscar—Gabby, Margot, Zora, and Sana.

"She gets the back," Oscar said, by now completely demoralized, feeling as though things could not get any worse. But of course, they could.

Like some hyper-alert social worker sensing a potential case of abuse, Margot gave Gabby a not-so-discreet look-over, head to toe. Whereas Zora and Sana wore matching floral-print dresses and shiny leather shoes with silver side buckles, Gabby wore grass-stained sneakers, striped leggings, and her prized "Save the Turtles" T-shirt, featuring a cartoon image of Sammy the Turtle. Worse still, the shirt now sported several splotches of what appeared to be raspberry jelly from the donut she had just eaten, and also a good amount of powdered sugar. Zora and Sana's dresses, Oscar noticed, were pristine—completely stain-free.

* * *

Ten minutes later, when father and daughter got into the Sorolla for the drive home, Oscar's mood wasn't so good. By any measure the morning had been a disaster. On a scale of one to ten, his chances with Margot were now likely … less than zero.

Bristling with self-anger—for whom else was there to blame?
—he buckled his seatbelt and said, "Well that was fun, huh?"

Missing the irony, the child nodded energetically and smiled.
"I like Zora and Sana. They're my new friends."

If there was one thing in this life that could lessen Oscar's ill-
temper, it was this: the sight of his daughter's happy face. Slowly,
a sort of half-smile came over his own face. "Good. I'm glad to
hear it."

Gabby then said, "Can they come to my birthday party?"

Oscar winced, the half-smile vanishing. His impulse was to
say no, to say it wasn't a good idea. But that wouldn't be fair to
the child. He let out a sigh, then said, "Sure ... If they want to."

FOUR

Over the next few days Oscar prepared for his mother's arrival, cleaning and rearranging his home. He and Gabby lived in the upper unit of a two family house that he and Lila had bought when they first moved to New Hampshire. The idea had been that the rent from the ground-floor unit would pay for Gabby's education. At the time, Lila was cancer-free and had just gotten a job with the Beauville School District as a music teacher. With their two incomes they could easily cover the home's mortgage, and the rental income would go into a college savings account. But within a year of taking possession of the house the cancer returned and Lila eventually had to leave her job. Since then, the rental income had been redirected toward the mortgage and other bills.

Recently, though, Oscar had begun to wonder if it wouldn't be best to sell the place: reduce his expenses, and maybe reduce the persistence of certain memories. The biggest of these concerned Lila's death. In her final weeks she had refused to go to a hospice. Instead she had made it clear that she wanted to die at home. She had loved the house and wanted to stay there till the end. Oscar had loved the house as well, and in many ways he still did. He and Lila had been happy there; not all the memories were painful.

And the place had much charm. It was an old house, built in the 1890s, and sat on a quiet street one block from a city park. It also had a large backyard. Coming from New York, where she had lived since college in a series of cramped apartments, Lila had especially wanted a lot of space so Gabby would be free to run and play and always be safe. Inside, the house had wood floors and high ceilings, and together husband and wife had repainted several of the rooms and built Oscar's attic studio.

Now, Oscar would be spending his nights in that studio, surrounded by stacks of canvases and the smell of drying oil paint. To make space for his mother in his bedroom he had cleared out some clothes from his closet and bureau and brought them up to the attic. To sleep on, he had set up an air mattress beside his easel. The situation wasn't ideal, but it was just temporary. In a week or so, he told himself, his mother would be gone and everything would go back to normal.

* * *

All too pleased to be rid of Stella Perilloux, Wickham Hill Assisted Living had offered to deliver her straight to Oscar's door. The plan had been for her to arrive early afternoon. But it wasn't until after four that a call came from the driver, saying they were here.

The van had parked in the driveway, and once outside Oscar saw his mother for the first time in two years. The last time had been at Beauville Hospital in the days following her operation. For fifty-plus years she had smoked and drank, and the result was cancer and the removal of half of one lung and a quarter of the other. Post-surgery, as she lay in bed recovering, Stella had asked Oscar to go get her a bottle of gin. He refused and she became irate. There were recriminations and nasty words, and in the end she told Oscar she never wanted to see him again. To which Oscar had said, "Fine."

Then, about a week ago, he got the call from Wickham Hill. A woman identifying herself as the retirement home's "Director of Resident Experience" explained the situation—namely, that Stella was getting the boot. Oscar asked how she had gotten his number. "Your brother; he told me to call you," the woman said. "Is this even legal?" Oscar said; "kicking an old woman out onto the street?" "Very legal," the Director of Resident Experience said; "Wickham Hill is a private entity. We take no federal or state funds. And your mother signed a terms of agreement contract. At last count she had a total of twenty-three personal-conduct violations. By a very wide margin, that is a Wickham Hill record." Oscar then called Duncan, who quickly became heated: "I'm done with her! I've had enough, Oscar. You do what you want." Twenty-four hours later, and with numerous misgivings, Oscar phoned his mother. He had called her twice before since her operation. Once on Christmas and once on her birthday. Both times she didn't answer; he left messages but she never called back. This time she picked up on the first ring. Oscar attempted some pleasantries, but she wasn't interested. Her responses were short and brusque. So he got right to it: if she wanted, she could stay temporarily with him in Beauville, and he would help her find a permanent place as soon as possible. But there was one condition: no drinking or smoking in front of Gabby. After he'd said this, there was a long silence. Then, in her gravelly smoker's voice, Stella said, "I suppose I could do that."

Now, the driver said, "Sorry we're late." He had just helped Stella out of the van. "Your mom wanted to make a few stops." The guy gave Oscar a meaningful look, and Oscar felt he understood: booze and nicotine, most likely.

With a plastic tube running from her nostrils down to an oxygen tank at her feet, Stella stood on the driveway, focusing on the house—and ignoring her son. She was a good-sized woman, broad-shouldered, full-busted, and now slightly stooped. She was seventy-three but looked more like ninety-three, with her face heavily lined and puffy beneath the eyes. Still scrutinizing the house, as though perhaps assessing its value, she said, "So this is it, huh?"

"Hello to you too, Ma. It's good to see you," Oscar said.

To this bit of sarcasm Stella said nothing. Instead her eyes brightened a touch and she made a faint smile, looking darkly amused. She was one of those rare people, Oscar felt, who seemed to revel in personal conflict. To *thrive* on it. Antagonizing others and giving offense, instigating scenes and provoking disputes—to Stella Perilloux, these were sources of great pleasure.

Beside the oxygen tank the driver set down an old American Tourister suitcase, now bulging, and a plastic carry-all bag, also bulging. "There you go," he said with an air of finality.

"That's everything?" Oscar said.

"Yep. That's it," the man said. Then, in a cheerier tone he added, "Take care, Stella."

She didn't even look at him.

With raised eyebrows and a droll expression, the driver gave Oscar a silent wave as if to say, "Good luck, buddy!" He got into the van, backed out of the driveway, and sped off.

Still focused on the house, Stella said, "I used to know someone who lived here. On the first floor. How long have you been here?"

"Five years. Since I moved back. We invited you for Thanksgiving the first year, but you didn't show up."

"I'm sure there was a good reason," she said, making another faint smile.

"I'm sure there was," Oscar said.

"And you own this? The whole thing?"

"Yes. We're upstairs."

"What do you get for the downstairs?"

"Fifteen-hundred a month."

"I'll give you seven hundred."

"That's a generous offer. But someone's already living there."

Stella smirked, though Oscar found its meaning unclear. She seemed either to be mocking him for having taken her offer seriously, or sneering resentfully because he had rejected it.

"Have you eaten?" he said.

"*No*," she said with sudden irritation. "I'm starving and I need a drink. *And don't worry*," she added gruffly, as if to shut him up, "I brought my own."

Patiently, Oscar said, "Ma, we already discussed this. I don't want you drinking in front of Gabby. After she goes to bed, fine. You can have … one or two. But not when she's up."

36

Stella glared at him. "What time does she go to bed?"

"Eight-thirty, nine."

"You expect me to wait till nine?"

"I do. Unless you want to sleep on the sidewalk tonight. And I'm not kidding. This is my house, Ma. My rules."

Stella looked him straight in the eye, her gaze flinty and shrewd. It was as though she was sizing him up, attempting to gauge his strengths and his weaknesses, and thereby calculate just how much mischief she might get away with.

"Come on," Oscar said. "Let's go up." He reached for her suitcase and bag, but she protested.

"I can take them myself," she growled. "I haven't made it this far in life by relying on the kindness of strangers."

It was a preposterous claim—not the second part but the first. The two bags appeared quite heavy, and either one alone would have been difficult for her to manage. And on top of this, there was her oxygen tank, which was fitted into a frame with wheels and required one hand to tow.

"I'll take these," Oscar said, "and you take your tank."

"Whatever you say," she grumbled. "I'm just a guest here."

* * *

She was a hard woman, Stella Perilloux. But this, Oscar felt, was because she had had a hard life. Born in Beauville as Stella McTavish, she had grown up very poor. Her truck-driver father had abandoned her and her mother, enlisted in the Army, and wound up dead in Korea, killed by a KPA sniper. Despite the abandonment, which happened when she was five, Stella always

regarded her father as a sainted war hero, and used his coura-
geous example as a weapon with which to belittle and shame
every other man in her life, none of whom could compare to
Corporal Joseph McTavish. By comparison, Stella's mother was,
in her daughter's words, "a drunk and a tramp." After Beauville
High, Stella worked briefly at the old Beauville Tannery until she
got pregnant by Buddy Boyle, a co-worker. The couple married,
produced Willie and Sarah, and then divorced after Buddy—as
if following the example of Corporal McTavish—abandoned *his*
family. Buddy's parents, who didn't think too highly of Stella, offered to raise the children, and Stella gladly accepted. She then
went to work at DeSanti's Supermarket, where she met Ronald
Perilloux, the deli counter supervisor. They married, had Duncan
and Oscar, and lived in a rented apartment on Prince Street near
the Beauville Library. One drunken summer afternoon, during
a family outing, Ronald Perilloux drowned in the Contoocook
River as his wife and kids watched from the shore. Oscar was
eight. Once again without a husband, Stella this time had no of-
fers for her children. She continued on at DeSanti's for another
seventeen years, then went to work at Sligo's Saloon, first as a
waitress, and later as the night manager. She stayed at Sligo's for
twenty-two years until age and emphysema lost her the job.

* * *

When Oscar and Stella entered the apartment Gabby was waiting to greet them.

"Hi Grammy!" the child cried. She was holding up a large
sheet of construction paper on which she had written, in different colored crayons, "Welcome to our house Grammy P.!!!" The

sign also included drawings of flowers and butterflies and waving monkeys with big smiles.

Startled, Stella stopped short. Her eyes fixed on the child and her face scrunched with distaste.

Just then Mindy the dog shot into the room, barking wildly at the intruder. The mini mutt beelined for Stella despite Gabby and Oscar shouting at her to stop.

"Hold that thing back or I'll kick him in the teeth!" Stella hollered.

"No!" Gabby shrieked.

Dropping the suitcase and bag, Oscar darted forward and scooped up the dog just feet away from Stella. He took her into Gabby's room, set her down, and shut the door. Outraged at this banishment, Mindy let loose another round of barking.

Back in the living room Oscar apologized to his mother, then went over to Gabby. Still holding the specially made sign, the child was frozen with fear, staring with stunned eyes at Grammy P. Oscar placed a comforting hand on her shoulder. "Grammy was just scared, that's all. She wasn't going to kick Mindy ... She didn't mean that ... *right?*" he added sharply, turning his now-hostile eyes on his mother.

Stella looked off to the side and raised her eyebrows as if to say, "That's what you think."

To Gabby Oscar said, "I thought we were going to keep Mindy in your room, with the door closed?"

"We were. But when you went downstairs I went into my room to look out the window to see Grammy and then I forgot to close the door."

"I see. Well, it's OK." To his mother he said, "Are you going to say hello to your granddaughter?"

Stella sighed, then gave the child a good once-over. "You've gotten big, Gabriella. Last time I saw you you were still a baby. You're a pretty girl." It was said matter-of-factly, a frank assessment rather than an attempt at flattery.

Gabby just watched the old woman, her little face still tense and afraid.

"You see?" Oscar said. "Grammy was just scared."

The child nodded and slowly seemed to relax. Pointing at the air tank, she said, "What's that?"

"That?" Stella said, looking down. "It's my boyfriend. Giovanni."

Gabby looked up at her father.

"She's joking. Old people think they're funny," he said. "The tank helps Grammy to breathe. There's air in it."

"Why does she need air?"

Because she smoked a pack of cigarettes a day for fifty years, Oscar thought. But he said, "Because she's sick."

Observing her Grammy, the strange woman who had just threatened to kick her dog in the teeth, Gabby grew silent, her watchful eyes somber and empathetic.

"Do you like the sign?" Oscar said, giving his mother a look.

She got the message. "Yes. It's nice."

Pleased at this, Gabby smiled.

* * *

Later, after she had unpacked some of her things and settled into her new room, Stella joined Oscar and Gabby in the kitchen. Oscar stood at the stove cooking while Gabby sat at the table, already set for supper. Without a word Stella wheeled her air tank over to the table and sat. She looked at Gabby for a few moments, said nothing, then looked around the kitchen taking everything in.

When Oscar set a plate in front of her, she eyed it with revulsion. "*What's this?*"

"Broccoli."

"I don't mean the broccoli! I mean the *other* thing, that vile orange thing."

"It's a veggie burger. It's good for you."

Stella glared at him, but Oscar said nothing. He set down Gabby's plate, then retrieved his own from the countertop and took his seat at the head of the table.

As if to explain, Gabby said, "I don't eat animals. Ms. Piroso says it's mean and bad for the environment." Ms. Piroso was Gabby's second-grade teacher at Lizzy Poppins Elementary.

Exploding with rage, a trait she shared with Duncan, Stella directed her venom at Oscar. "Well I *do* eat animals! Every day of my life I eat animals!"

"I still eat meat myself," he said calmly. "But Gabby doesn't. She eats fish, but that's it. Tomorrow I'll make us some chicken."

Stella shook her head, fuming. "Does she tell you when you can go potty too?"

"*Ma*—watch it."

More head shaking from Stella. "If your grandfather could see this … The man took a bullet for this country! *And for what?*"

"I know, Ma. I know. Now just try it. It's good."

Stella looked at her plate and wrinkled her nose, as if detecting a foul odor. Then, defiantly, she passed over the veggie burger and took a bite of her broccoli. Next came a forkful of rice. And at last, a tiny bite of the veggie burger. Aware that she was being watched, she wrinkled her lips with displeasure.

"It's tasty, right?" Oscar said.

Stella shrugged, then admitted, "It's OK." She took another, larger bite of the veggie burger, and then another.

Gabby said, "Grammy, do you watch *The Wild Life with Jamie and Gina* on the computer?"

"Never heard of it," Stella said, working on her food.

"It's my favorite show."

"Is that right."

"Yep. Last night I watched and Jamie and Gina did an experiment to see how smart honey badgers are. And you wanna know what? Honey badgers are almost as smart as monkeys." The child gazed expectantly at her Grammy.

"Kind of like your Uncle Duncan," Stella said, taking another bite of broccoli.

Gabby giggled. "No, people are smarter than monkeys. But you wanna know how they did the experiment? They had a trap and they put some food in it, and the honey badger had to figure out how to open the trap to get the food. Do you know what food they used?"

"Let me guess—honey?"

Gabby was amazed. "Did you watch it too?"

Stella shot Oscar an annoyed glance, as if to say, "Does this kid ever shut up?"

"Gabby, come on, eat," he said. "If you finish all your food, maybe after supper you can play something for Grammy on the piano." Gabby had been playing the instrument since age three, and was now pretty good. At least, to Oscar's ear she was pretty good.

For her part, Stella seemed less than enthused at the prospect of a private musical recital. "My shows start at seven-thirty," she said.

"Your shows?" Oscar said.

"*Lucky Dice Rollers*, then *Zach and BooBoo* at eight. And *Love Detectives* at nine."

"We can only watch TV on Saturday," Gabby said helpfully, and maybe with a hint of bossiness. She might be young, her attitude seemed to say, but this was still her turf.

"Well I can watch TV *every day!*" Stella fired back, once again losing her cool and turning on Oscar. "This is America, not Russia!"

With an air of injured righteousness, Gabby likewise turned on Oscar. She said nothing but her expression, grave and resolute, made it clear that she expected her father to step in and lay down the law.

Patience slipping, Oscar told himself to remain calm. In the Perilloux home television was a sensitive topic. From day one Lila had decided that Gabby would not watch TV until age five or six, and thereafter only sparingly. She had read research on the subject, about the various harmful effects of television on young minds, both emotional and physiological, and felt very strongly about it. She also wanted to shield the child from what she called the "sewer" of most popular culture. Oscar, who had been raised on *Sesame Street* and afterschool reruns of *The Love Boat, Gilligan's Island,* and *The Simpsons,* had thought her views a bit extreme. But as with most things related to Gabby, Oscar had deferred to his wife and her ten-plus years of teaching experience. And in time he was glad that he had, as he had grown to see the wisdom of her ideas. Lately though Gabby had begun to rebel. Hearing from her cousin Bonnie and various other schoolmates about certain shows on cable and network TV, including *Sexy Teen Showdown,* the child had begun to campaign for a loosening of the rules. Oscar held firm, but he was beginning to waver. Currently the rule was that Gabby could watch PBS kids' shows on Saturday morning along with a kids' movie on Saturday night. The rest of the week her viewing was restricted to educational videos on the internet—such as *The Wild Life with Jamie and Gina,* a children's nature series focused on animals and the environment. But for how much longer could he keep the world out of his home, Oscar wondered? For how much longer could he maintain his child's innocence?

With a sigh, and knowing there would be some blowback, he said, "Grammy can watch TV tonight. She's a guest here."

Gabby's brow furrowed crossly, and for some moments she seemed to ponder the justice of this decision, questioning if it was fair that a guest could watch TV during the week but not her. Then, as though having reached her decision, she pouted her lips, ignored her father's eye, and silently went back to her food.

* * *

After supper Stella went into the living room to watch her shows, while Oscar and Gabby remained in the kitchen to clean up. As she did every night, Gabby got out the stool from the broom closet, set it before the sink, stepped up onto it, and started washing dishes. Oscar cleared the table and wiped down the stove.

Over the sound of the running water the child said, "How long is Grammy going to live here again?"

"I don't know," Oscar said. "We'll see."

* * *

Most weeknights following kitchen cleanup Gabby would spend a half hour on the piano practicing the week's lesson for her teacher Mrs. Molina, and afterward spend a half hour on the computer up in Oscar's studio watching one of her videos. Tonight, however, there would be no music. The piano, an old secondhand upright, the best Oscar could afford, was in the living room along with the television. Rather than provoke another argument with his mother Oscar felt the best move was to get the child directly on the computer.

But as father and daughter entered the living room on their way to the stairs up to the attic, they saw an incredible sight. Seated on the sofa watching *Lucky Dice Rollers*—a euphoric contestant suddenly cried out, "*Snake eyes! Snake eyes! Snake eyes!*" —Stella exhaled a swirling plume of white vapor. In one hand she held a highball glass, and in the other an electric cigarette. As the plume faded then disappeared, the room filled with the sweet fragrance of strawberries. In the air as well Oscar noted a faint whiff of gin.

Gabby was the first to speak. "What's that?" she said, eyeing the cigar-shaped metal tube in her grandmother's hand.

Unfazed by the appearance of her hosts, and with the air tank at her side and the plastic tubes up her nose, Stella said, "Grammy's medicine." A wry smile came over her face.

Oscar was struck dumb, unable to speak.

"It smells good," Gabby said. "Can I try it?"

"*No!*" Oscar blurted out, at last finding his words. "No!"

Gabby looked up at him, alarmed by his strong feeling.

"No," Oscar repeated in a gentler tone, catching himself. "Grammy's … *medicine* is dangerous. It's like poison. Don't ever touch it. You'll get very sick."

"How come she doesn't get sick?"

"She *does* get sick … Just look at—"

"Your daddy's right, Gabriella," Stella said calmly, cutting Oscar off. "This is bad for little girls. And it tastes terrible."

A doubtful expression came over Gabby's face. "It smells good," she repeated.

"Come on," Oscar said, placing a hand on her back to lead her away. "Let's get you on the computer."

As they crossed the room Gabby said, "What's this show?" Her eyes were now fastened on the TV. A contestant had just rolled the large fuzzy dice and was maniacally yelling *"Big money! Big money!"* as the audience wildly cheered.

"Can we watch it?" the child said.

"No."

* * *

Once Gabby was settled in, seated at the desktop computer with headphones on, watching the screen as Jamie and Gina commenced another adventure—this one in Australia with kangaroos—Oscar headed back downstairs. His first stop was Gabby's room. It was time to let the dog out. He opened the door and scooped up Mindy. As master and mutt passed through the living room, which still smelled faintly of strawberries, the dog barked at Stella with eye-bulging ferocity. Ignoring his mother, Oscar made no attempt to shush the dog. They proceeded to the kitchen and then down the stairs to the backyard, where Oscar clipped Mindy to her runner. Still in a frenzy, the tiny fighter began barking wildly all around, as if daring any nearby foe to step forward and take a thrashing. But as no foe took up the challenge, the dog soon fell silent, and now looked bored.

Thinking of his own foe, Oscar inhaled a deep breath of the cool night air and marched back upstairs and into the living room. Stella looked at him, the television still blaring. She had lost the e-cigarette but was still clutching her glass.

Though he was in a fury Oscar felt his rage suddenly ebb. Seeing his mother in her decrepit state, with the air tank and the nose tubes, the white hair and the wrinkled skin, stabbed him with something like pity. He took the TV remote from the coffee table, lowered the volume, then said, more with pleading than anger, "What the hell are you thinking, smoking in front of her?"

"It's not smoking. It's vaping! And it's very safe. All the kids are doing it."

"I know what it is, Ma. I know what vaping is. The question is why are you doing it in this house, in front of my daughter?"

"You never said I couldn't!" she said, affronted.

"Yeah, and I never said you couldn't burn the house down either, but that doesn't mean you can."

Stella looked away, shaking her head. "Listen to this one," she muttered to the wall. "So dramatic."

"And the drinking," Oscar went on. "I told you when you got here—I *specifically* told you—*no drinking* until she goes to bed. And yet here you are, sipping away like this is Sligo's Saloon."

"You need to lighten up, you know that?" Stella griped. "Jesus, you sound just like your brother!"

That stung a bit, and gave Oscar pause. He had always been the easygoing one to Duncan's high-stress tight-ass. Growing up he had laughed when Stella told bawdy jokes to the neighborhood kids, whereas Duncan had turned red with shame. Oscar had been friendly with Stella's boyfriends, while Duncan was always frosty. Oscar had done his fair share of high school drinking and pot-smoking, but Duncan didn't drink till college.

Stella said, "I hid the bottle, OK? As far as the kid was concerned I was drinking water."

"Is that right," Oscar said, the anger rising up again. "Duncan and I knew you weren't drinking water, back in the day. Nine, ten years old, we knew what you were up to."

Stella made a putout face, as though Oscar was being a pain in the ass, or worse—a prig.

"The point, Ma, is that I told you not to do it, and yet you did. Your first night here and already you're up to your shenanigans. I'm telling you, I don't want Gabby exposed to this crap."

"*What crap?*"

"The drinking, the smoking, the TV on all day. All the stuff that we were exposed to as kids."

"*Ooooh*, I see! Here we go!" Stella cried out. "The victim, is that it? Trust me, I've heard it all before—for *years* I heard your brother whining about his childhood. The poor baby! Well let me tell *you* something, kid: you turned out OK and so did Duncan, with all his millions. And what thanks do *I* get? *Zippo*, that's what. After your father died, who was it that kept that house running? Who put food on the table? *Me*, just me. With no help from his family, those white-trash Perillouxs. A bunch of drunks, all of them."

"OK, Ma. You kept the house running. Whatever you say. But right now what we're talking about is you not vaping or drinking in front of Gabby. It's nice out now, so if you have to do it, you can vape all you want out on the back deck after she goes to school, and then at night after she goes to bed. And the same for the drinking. You do what you have to do, but don't do it in front of her … Do you understand?"

Scowling, Stella made no reply.

"Do you *understand?*" Oscar repeated.

"Fine," she said, meeting his eye. "Whatever you say."

FIVE

They were playing basketball, a mix of men and teenagers. One of the men, a tall heavyset guy in a green Celtics jersey and a white terrycloth headband that read, "The Banger," had the ball out beyond the three-point arc. Between him and the basket was a blur of action—bodies dashing in all directions, sneakers squeaking on the hardwood floor. One of the Banger's teammates, a skinny kid with braces, was waving a hand and calling out, "*I'm open! I'm open!*" Ignoring the kid—who indeed was open—the Banger launched the ball toward the basket. Several of the guys groaned; one laughed. Missing the hoop entirely, the ball caromed off the backboard with a pitiful thud. Amid the scrum for the rebound Oscar rose up high and snatched the ball. He rose up again and knocked down a five-foot jumper.

Running back to the other end of the court, the skinny kid with braces muttered, "Nice shot Walter."

Walter—aka Walter Bang—said, "It was a pass, genius. Now stop whining and play some D you lazy twerp."

Not breaking his stride the kid said, "Look who's talking."

A faint grin came over Walter's face, no doubt because the kid had a point. While everyone else was running to get into position, Walter was walking, slow as a turtle.

Already on the attack, one of the opposing guards zipped a pass to a guy at the top of the key. The guy faked right, then drove left to the hoop and pulled up short for an eight-footer. The ball hit the top of the rim, bounced up high. Oscar timed his jump, came down with the ball, then fired a football pass the other way, catching Walter as he broke for the opposite basket.

Unopposed, Walter laid the ball in for an easy bucket. With a gloating smirk he turned back to the others and bellowed, "That's the game, ladies! Have a good night."

* * *

Most Thursdays after five Oscar would meet up with Walter for pickup basketball at the Y, followed by a burger and a couple beers at the Beauville Brewhouse. At Beauville High they had played varsity sports together—football, basketball, baseball— and had generally got up to no good. Walter's dad, "Big Walter," had owned a small market on West Street called Big Walter's Provisions. The place sold the basics—bread, milk, scratch tickets, Twinkies—but also had a massive beer cooler that young Walter would discreetly raid on weekend nights. The spoils of such petty thefts had been generously shared, leading to the intoxication of many Beauville teenagers. Oscar himself had drunk numerous "brewskis" courtesy of Big Walter's unwitting generosity. A big kid and a decent athlete, young Walter, already known as "The Banger," was brash and loud, a bit of a card, a guy's guy. From Beauville High he went on to Plymouth State College, where he flunked out after one brief but memorable booze-filled year. There had been blackouts and pranks and all sorts of debauchery. Returning to Beauville he married a local girl and later took over Big Walter's Provisions, after an aneurysm struck Big Walter dead one night at the Beauville Bowl-O-Rama. Now, twenty years later, Walter still ran the market but his marriage was history. One day without warning his wife had announced that she was leaving him. She said she "wanted more out of life," and that was that. His two sons, now grown—one was currently in the Army and stationed in Iraq, the other was enrolled at a cooking school in Chicago—were rarely in touch. Occasionally, by the second or third beer, Walter would hint at his loneliness and his many regrets, and speak openly of how he missed the old days —the days of his and Oscar's youth, when everything had been so much better …

Tonight, though, the conversation was centered very much on the present. Over their burgers and fries Oscar told Walter about his mother: her expulsion from Wickham Hill Assisted Living, her arrival at his place, the vaping, the gin, the threat to kick Mindy in the teeth.

Walter was grinning. "Old Mrs. P—she always was a character. I remember back in the day, when you were down in Philly, she got into it with my old man. Really gave him hell."

"What happened?"

"Well … I don't know," Walter said, hesitating.

"It's fine," Oscar said. "Tell me."

"She nicked a bottle of wine, at the store."

"What?"

"Yeah. She comes in and picks out a few things, and at the cash register Big Walter says, 'You plan on paying for that bottle you put in your bag?' And just like that she goes into a rage, denying everything but refusing to open her bag. Big Walter says, 'I saw you do it; I saw you in the mirror,' and then she tears into him, calling him all sorts of names. Now as you know, my father didn't take shit from anyone. He kept a baseball bat *and* a gun behind the counter, and over the years I saw him use both on different occasions. And when he did, he did it with a smile on his face —Clint Eastwood style. But with your mom he stood down. I don't know, it was probably because you and I were buddies. He just told her to leave and not come back."

Oscar shook his head. "I knew nothing about this. Why didn't you tell me?"

"Because by that point you were gone, and I didn't see you again for what, fifteen years? It's old news."

"I'm sorry. It's embarrassing."

"Forget it. Like I said, old news."

Warily Oscar said, "Is there anything else you know about? Stuff that happened when I was gone?" Once he'd left for college, Oscar rarely returned home. Beauville was a place he just wanted to forget.

Walter vacillated.

"What?" Oscar said.

"After Big Walter passed and I took over the store, your mom started coming back in ..."

"Go on."

"She started running a tab. At first it was ten, twenty bucks a week. Then it started to go up. But she was clever about it," Walter said, now with a mirthful look in his eye. "What she'd do is, she'd come in, give me ten bucks toward the bill, but then she'd stock up on groceries and booze and add another twenty, thirty dollars to the tab. For months this goes on, and by now the total is up to five, six hundred bucks, and I'm thinking there's going to be another scene, like the one with Big Walter, and that's the last damn thing I want. So what I do is, I call your brother. Even then he had plenty of cash. And he took care of it."

"What'd he do?"

"He came to the store, paid off the debt, and added another five hundred on top of it. He told me to call him when she'd gone through it, and that he'd give me another five hundred. He was very decent about it. Dunc's a good man. A little full of himself, but maybe he's earned it."

Their waitress came up to them. As always they were sitting in a booth, away from the noisy bar. Dressed in skin-tight yoga pants and a plaid mini-blouse that revealed lots of skin, including a pierced navel and much of her plump bosom, the young woman asked if they wanted anything else.

"For some reason I'm thinking of melons," Walter said with a mischievous grin. "Do you have anything melon-y?"

A ripple of irritation passed over the waitress's face, and then a look of boredom. She ignored the comment and turned to Oscar.

"Another round," he said. "Thank you."

The girl walked off and Walter followed with his eyes.

"I think that was a mistake," Oscar said.

"Nah. That's just Pam. She knows I was kidding."

* * *

54

Halfway through their last round Oscar said, "Let me ask you something. Can you tell that I cut my own hair?"

Walter laughed. "Are you kidding?"

"No."

"Well, sure. I thought either it was you, or maybe your barber has Parkinson's."

"It's that bad?"

"I didn't say *bad*. It's just, you know, a little eccentric ... Kind of a cross between Keith Richards and the Beverly Hillbillies."

"That's very flattering. I'm trying to save money. Things are tight. I cut Gabby's hair too."

Walter nodded, sipped his beer. "Why do you ask?"

"Well ... There's this woman."

"Oh! That's great. Who is she?"

"Her name is Margot," Oscar said, and he spilled the whole story: about how he had first seen her at church, and how he'd met her at the softball game, and how she was seeing Duncan.

"Well, I'm glad to hear it," Walter said. "I've been wondering when you were going to get back out there. Maybe it's time, you know? But Duncan? As your rival? ... Hmmm, let's see: he's rich, successful, and good looking. As for you, well—you've got an interesting haircut. And now your mother lives with you."

"You're a funny guy, Walter."

"Look, big picture? This is a good thing. A very good thing—the juices are starting to flow again and you're ready to move on. But my advice? Look elsewhere. Find a different girl."

* * *

Oscar returned home just after nine. Opening the front door he heard loud rhythmic music and cheering voices. The racket was coming from the second floor, from his living room. Gym bag in hand, he quietly strode up the stairs, not wanting to announce his arrival. From the archway by the top of the stairs he peered into the living room.

Seated side by side on the sofa, Stella and Gabby were staring at the television, transfixed. On the screen a man and a woman, both projecting unnatural, maniacal smiles, strutted and shimmied and twirled to the music's frenetic beat. In each of their hands, Stella and Gabby held a spoon and a bowl of ice cream. On the coffee table was an empty carton of peppermint crunch.

"You guys having fun?" Oscar said.

Gabby's head whipped around and her eyes showed lots of white—a picture of pure panic. Stella, with far less urgency, also looked over at Oscar. Her expression was unbothered; placid, even.

Oscar said to her, "Would you mind turning that down." It was an order, not a request.

Stella set her bowl on the coffee table, picked up the remote, and decreased the volume. Oscar then focused on his daughter. Trembling with worry, Gabby lowered her gaze and jutted out her bottom lip, looking as though she was going to burst into tears. Oscar actually felt sorry for her.

He said, "Where's Mackenzie?" Mackenzie was the child's regular babysitter. Earlier, before he had left for the Y, Oscar had told Mackenzie—in front of Stella—to make sure Gabby stuck to her normal routine: supper, dishes, a half hour on the piano, a half hour on the computer, a bath, then bed.

"She went home," Gabby said.

"She went home," Oscar repeated.

Gabby nodded, and again her bottom lip jutted out.

"When?" Oscar said, directing the question to Stella.

"A couple hours ago. She wasn't needed."

Oscar told himself to relax; the fury was building. "Is that right."

There was no answer.

"Was she paid?"

"*I* didn't give her any money," Stella snapped. "She wasn't my babysitter!"

Knowing he was about to erupt, Oscar decided the best thing was for him to step away. To Gabby he said, "OK, come on. Let's get you ready for bed."

* * *

In the child's room, Oscar shut the door. The space was small and cluttered. Toys and books and stuffed animals were scattered about, along with clothes and sneakers and shoes. The room had its own unique scent, its Gabby scent, and something about it always comforted Oscar. The two of them sat on the edge of her bed.

"So what happened tonight?" he said gently. "Grammy told Mackenzie to go home?"

The child nodded, silent and gloomy-faced.

"Was Grammy nice to Mackenzie?"

Another nod, this time with an earnest, helpful expression. "Grammy said she could take care of me, and Mackenzie could come back another time."

"OK ... And what about the ice cream and the TV—I thought I said we would only do that on Saturday nights?" In addition to the one-night-per-week rule on TV watching, there was also a one-night-per-week rule on eating ice cream.

The gloomy face returned, and Gabby said, "We did."

"What happened?"

The child stiffened. "Grammy said it was OK."

"She did, huh?"

Gabby nodded.

"She said you could eat ice cream and watch TV," Oscar said, to clarify.

Another nod.

"And did you tell her that you're not supposed to do those things on a Thursday night?"

The child hesitated.

"Gabby?"

"Yes. I told her," she said, now looking very sad. "Am I in trouble?"

Oscar sighed. Obviously, his mother had instigated the whole affair, not Gabby. Yet if he let this slide, the child disobeying him when he was away, who knows what she might get up to next? He said, "You did break the rules. And that's not good ... On the other hand, Grammy was in charge and she said you could ... So this is what we're going to do. No ice cream this Saturday. And from now on, no TV unless I say. Period. I'm your father, not Grammy. OK?"

Another nod, the child suddenly less sad. She said, "Is Grammy in trouble?"

"That's between her and me … But how did things go after Mackenzie left? With Grammy?"

The child glowed with delight, her emotions shifting yet again. "It was fun," she said brightly. "On this one show that we watched, you can win money if you pick the right letters and guess the words. One time Grammy guessed before everyone else. If she was on the show she would have won about five hundred dollars!"

"Really."

"Mm-hm. And on this other show, the one we were watching just now, people do a dance and everyone cheers, and if they get the most points, they can win. Though I don't know what they can win. I have to ask Grammy. It was really good though. Can we watch it again?"

Wearily, Oscar raised a hand to his face and began rubbing his eyes. There were many thoughts swirling in his mind just then —none of which had anything to do with TV. "I don't know," he said. "We'll see."

* * *

After he tucked Gabby in, Oscar returned to the living room for another confrontation with his mother. But Stella had already cleared out. The television was off and the bowls and the ice-cream carton were gone. Oscar checked her room, then the kitchen, and finally found her out on the back deck.

With the air tank at her side, she was seated on a plastic yard chair under the glow of a single halogen bulb. In one hand was her glass of gin, in the other her e-cig. As Oscar opened the screen door and stepped out beside her, Stella averted her head and exhaled a plume of strawberry-scented vapor. In her gruff gravelly voice she said, "You should get one of those bug zappers. I'm getting eaten alive out here." To drive home the point she set down her glass and slapped her opposite arm, as though to squash a pesky mosquito.

But Oscar was in no mood to discuss insects. He said, "Ma, what happened tonight is unacceptable. It's *unacceptable!*—" Abruptly, he paused: had he really just said "It's unacceptable"? Since when, Oscar wondered, had he become the kind of person who says "It's unacceptable"? He continued, saying, "I wanted the babysitter here for a reason, and that was to make sure you didn't pull one of your stunts!"

Stella made no reply. With a cool unruffled air she sipped her gin, keeping her focus not on her son but on the darkened yard. In the distance a dog was barking.

Oscar said, "Were you drinking and vaping in front of Gabby tonight?"

"No, and it was killing me. I've had the shakes and the sweats for two damn hours."

This was unexpected. That his mother was both an alcoholic and a nicotine addict was no surprise. But that she would half-admit to this—that was new. At least, in their very limited contact over the last twenty-plus years, Oscar had never heard her admit to any dependencies of any sort. When she had first got the cancer diagnosis, she told him, "I can stop whenever I want; I smoke because I enjoy it. These doctors can go screw themselves."

"Have you thought about quitting?" he said. "Or cutting back?"

For the first time since she'd arrived, four days ago, his mother gave him what appeared to be an open, forthright look—though it came with a droll smirk. "It's too late for that," she said.

"No it isn't. We could get you some help."

She chortled, dismissing the idea, then took another drag off her e-cig.

"Ma, the woman at Wickham Hill told me you might have trouble finding a new home to take you in. The drinking and the smoking are a problem. And because of your financial situation, your choices are going to be pretty limited."

"Is that right."

"Yes."

"And what else did she say?" Stella said, with a mix of defiance and derision.

"Well, for one thing she said you were running a rigged card game. And that you were using the money to get booze and cigarettes from some of the orderlies. Apparently two of them got fired because of it. Is this true?"

"It's called free enterprise. I needed the money and I did what I had to do. If Duncan wasn't so damn cheap, none of this would've happened."

"I see. It's Duncan's fault. Even though he got you into a luxury retirement home and paid ten grand a month for what, two years? Three years?"

Stella shot back: "Did you ever ask him why he sent me so far north? Two hours from Beauville? Even though there are plenty of nice homes around here?"

Oscar was silent.

"It's because he wanted me out of town. I embarrass him, he said. I've *always* embarrassed him, he said. He also made sure all of my Social Security money went into paying the bill. It wasn't all just him, as he likes to tell everybody. And he did it on purpose, so I wouldn't have anything left over. So yes, it *is* his fault. He's got more money than Rockefeller. He could have easily left me with my twelve hundred a month." Twelve-hundred was the amount of her monthly Social Security checks.

"I didn't know any of that," Oscar said. "But either way, Ma, he told me he's not going to help you anymore. And I think he means it."

She waved a hand, both bitter and resigned. "I'm sure I'll end up on the streets."

"That won't happen. Tomorrow I'll make some calls. I was going to do it today but I got busy with other things. I'm sure we'll find something. Maybe something here in Beauville. In the meantime, Ma, if you're going to stay here, you need to start following my rules. Now I told you, very specifically, that I don't want Gabby watching TV, and yet—"

"*Oh for God's sake!*" Stella roared, her eyes filling with rage. "Let the kid have some fun. You run this place like a goddamn concentration camp! It's suffocating! Really, between you and that brother of yours, I don't know who's worse. Two uptight fuddy-duddies. Trust me, you were never like this as a kid."

Oscar remained calm. He wasn't going to take the bait. His mother's life was a mess and she was looking for someone to blame, looking for someone to have it out with, but he wasn't going to give her the satisfaction. Very reasonably he replied, "Like I said, Ma: tomorrow I'll make some calls. Good night."

SIX

Oscar was having trouble focusing on the Mass. As the reader read the readings, as the organist played the music, and as Father Butler gave the homily and performed the ancient rites, he found his eye crossing the aisle again and again.

Flanked by her twins, Margot Saadeh was installed in her usual spot. Installed in *his* usual spot, Oscar was hoping Margot might turn around and send him a smile or a friendly nod, let him know that last Sunday's coffee-social awkwardness was forgotten, or at least forgiven. But Margot's focus remained firmly on the service. Even during the Sign of Peace, the moment in the Mass when congregants shake hands with those around them, she had kept her eyes away from Oscar. This, he felt, was not good. Surely she had decided he was someone best to avoid, a pathetic figure in need of not a new friend but a therapist, a hairstylist, and a stack of parenting manuals.

Mercifully, Father Butler gave his final blessing and the Mass was ended. Oscar leaned over to Gabby and whispered, "Let's go." He wanted to slip out quick, get back to the car and on the road before the rest of the congregation had finished singing the exit hymn.

Gabby, however, had other ideas. With a look of distress she said, "But I want to invite Zora and Sana to my birthday party."

Oscar winced. The child's birthday was the following Saturday, and Oscar had already told her she could invite the twins. "OK," he said. "We'll wait."

After the organ played the morning's final note and folks began filing out, Gabby went up the aisle to greet Zora and Sana, still in their pew. The kids talked, then turned to Margot. Words were exchanged. A concerned expression came over Margot's face and she looked over at Oscar, who had remained seated. He waved and managed a stiff smile. Margot likewise waved and managed a stiff smile.

The four females, three little, one big, made their way down the center aisle. Oscar joined them and they all headed for the exit. Margot asked about the party and Oscar explained that it was going to be small, about seven or eight girls. There would be pony rides at a local farm, followed by a sleepover at Oscar's with pizza and a movie.

Margot looked uneasy.

"Bonnie's coming," Oscar added, thinking that might reassure her.

But the comment seemed to have the opposite effect. Margot frowned, and fell silent. Clearly she was having some doubts.

The twins, however, were all in.

"Mom I wanna go! I wanna ride a pony!" one of them said.

"I wanna go too!" the other one said. "A pony, a pony!"

"Mom, a pony!"

"Mom, Mom!"

"OK, OK," Margot relented, though she didn't look too pleased about it.

The girls cheered and Gabby beamed.

As they stepped out into the bright sunlight, Gabby said to the twins, "Are you guys going to the coffee thing?"

The twins looked up at their mother and said, in stereo: "Can we go to the coffee thing?"

Margot wavered. "I … I don't think today—"

"I want a donut!" one of the girls said.

"I want a donut too!" the other one said.

"Mom!"

"Mom!"

"Fine—let's get a donut," Margot grumbled.

"Daddy can we get a donut?" Gabby asked.

"Uh … sure. Why not?"

* * *

"I should get your number," Margot said.

"My number?" Oscar said.

"Yes, for the party."

"Oh. I thought you were getting fresh."

Margot flinched, and her eyes narrowed. Observing Oscar she appeared perplexed, as though she was wondering if he had just said something witty, or offensive. She said nothing.

The two of them, once again, were in the church hall, each holding a hot coffee in a paper cup. Oscar was cheery, and hopeful. This was a chance at redemption, a chance to redeem last Sunday's poor showing. And really, what did he have to lose? In his mother's words: *zippo*. He said, "But yes, it's a good idea. I can text you the directions."

After they exchanged numbers, Margot looked at him. Remarkably, there was a playful glimmer in her eyes. A merry sparkle. It was as though she had decided she was open to the possibility of a little banter; open to the idea of maybe giving him a second chance. She said, "What is it with girls and ponies?"

Not missing a beat, Oscar said, "The danger."

Margot laughed; Oscar felt giddy.

"I remember I wanted one," she said. "Very badly."

"Did you get one?"

"No. In fact, I've never even ridden one."

"Well, then Saturday's your big chance."

This drew another laugh. He was on a roll.

They talked more about the party and soon the three girls swarmed around them, each of the kids eating a donut.

Gabby said, "Daddy, Zora and Sana never rode a pony before. They're from Manhattan, and they don't have ponies there."

Chewing on their treats, the twins looked up at Oscar and nodded, as if to verify this unfortunate fact.

"Well, it's fun," Oscar said. "You girls are going to have a great time."

* * *

That evening at supper Gabby was in full curiosity mode. Following her illicit night of TV and ice cream, the child had developed a great liking for her Grammy. This was only reinforced by the two of them playing a game of Parcheesi on Friday evening, and by Stella joining in on Gabby and Oscar's Saturday movie night. The three of them had sat on the sofa, sans ice cream, and watched *Toy Story*, which Stella seemed to enjoy even though Gabby kept giving away the plot. In fact over the past few days the only glitch in domestic harmony had come when Mindy the dog peed on one of Stella's shirts, which she had left on the floor in her room.

The child said, "Grammy, you're Daddy's mother, right?"

"That's what they tell me," Stella said, biting into her meatless burrito.

"And where did you guys live, in the olden days?"

"Over on Prince Street, near the library."

"Wait—you lived in Beauville?"

"We did. A big happy family."

"You didn't live in New York?"

"No. Your daddy moved there after college, I believe."

"*I* was born in New York," Gabby said proudly.

"Impressive," Stella said, taking another bite.

"Gabby, eat," Oscar said.

The child bit into her burrito, chewed meditatively, then said, "What was my daddy like when he was little?"

"Your daddy? He was a hell-raiser," Stella said. "Him and that Walter Bang and that LaCroix kid. I'm surprised they didn't all end up in jail."

"Ma …"

"Uncle Walter?" Gabby said.

"*Uncle Walter?*" Stella said, now looking at Oscar.

"Yeah. We've reconnected."

"What's a 'hell-raiser'?" Gabby said.

"Someone who's a pain in the butt," Stella said. "When your daddy and his brother were little, I'd take the belt to them, chase 'em all through the house."

Remembering this—remembering the wildness of his up-bringing, the mischief and the occasional instances of maternal retribution—Oscar smiled. But Gabby was lost. Not once in her brief life had she been hit or whipped by either Oscar or Lila, and so the concept of being chased by a belt-wielding parent did not compute. "Why did you have a belt?" she said. "Because they wouldn't get dressed?"

"*What?*" Stella croaked, her mouth half full with food.

"How come you had a belt?"

"Gabby, let Grammy eat," Oscar said.

The doorbell rang, and immediately Mindy erupted, barking in a mad fury.

"That damn dog!" Stella said.

"It's probably some political canvassers," Oscar said. New Hampshire's presidential primary was slated for the following February, which meant the state was already crawling with can-didates and operatives and hordes of college kids going door to door.

"Why don't you sic Mindy on 'em, give her something to do," Stella said.

Again the doorbell rang, and again Mindy went into a frenzy.

"Here we go!" Stella said.

Oscar pushed back his chair, went into the living room, scooped up the dog, tossed her into Gabby's room, shut the door, then went down the stairs as the bell rang yet again.

It wasn't a young canvasser, or even a candidate. Instead it was an older man, about Stella's age, with a haggard red face and a prominent belly, the lower part of which was exposed beneath the bottom of his white T-shirt. He had humble eyes and a nervous expression. Standing on the porch, returning Oscar's gaze, the man looked uncomfortable, as though he was expecting trouble, or rejection. But when Oscar gave him a polite "Hello," the man's eyes brightened a touch and he seemed to relax. "Hello there," he said. "I've come to see Stell."

"Excuse me?"

"I've come to see Stella. Your mom."

Almost unthinkingly, Oscar gave the man another gander: The humble, cautious eyes. The cheeks red with burst capillaries, most likely from booze. The roll of exposed belly flab.

"And how do you know my mother?"

"Well ... We're involved."

" 'Involved'?"

"Stella's my girl."

Oscar gaped. After a pause he said, "I see ..." He then extended his hand, saying, "I'm Oscar."

At this gesture of goodwill, the man smiled with appreciation. "I know," he said.

"Have we met?"

"No. But I've known your mother since before you were born. And when you were a kid I used to look for your name in the paper. You were quite the football player. Pretty good at basketball and baseball too. And you played football at that college in Pennsylvania."

"That's right," Oscar said, fairly astonished.

This little exchange seemed to gratify the man and boost his confidence. With a newfound sense of dignity he said, "Harold Buckett. The pleasure is all mine." His tone was formal, almost courtly, and he even made a slight bow.

Baffled at this, Oscar half wondered if the guy was putting him on. But he said, "It's great to meet you, Harold ... Come on in. We're just finishing supper."

* * *

When the two men entered the kitchen Stella groaned.

"What the hell are you doing here?" she said.

"*Ma!*"

"I came to see you, Stell. We need to talk."

"No we don't! That's why I stopped calling you, remember?"

"Ma, please—"

"I miss you, Stell. I can't live without you."

"Well I can live without you you old drunk, that's for damn sure!"

"Don't say that, Stell. Don't be cruel."

At this Stella went silent, and she looked away.

"You know I love you," Harold said. "And I'm proud to say it in front of your family."

Gabby's little eyes had gone round with wonder. Taking everything in, every word, every gesture, she was spellbound. Never before had she seen such drama.

Oscar said, "Look, this is a discussion the two of you need to have elsewhere. Either that, Harold, or you're going to have to leave."

Harold focused his pleading gaze on the object of his misery. "Stell," he said.

Aware that all eyes were now fixed on her, Stella seemed to bloom under the attention. A regal look came over her. With a haughty air she raised her chin and mugged with queenly disdain. Avoiding Harold's eye, she prolonged the silence, making it very clear who was master here. At last she said, "I suppose we could talk."

Finished with her meatless burrito, Stella rose from her chair, towed her air tank around the table, and started down the short hallway to the bedrooms. Harold followed.

"Ah, *excuse me*," Oscar called out. "What are you doing?"

Stella looked back. "Going to my room."

Recalling Harold's statement—"Stella's my girl"—Oscar said, "Oh no you're not." The thought of his mother and Harold Buckett having make-up sex, or some such activity, in *this house*, was not going to happen. No, no, no. No way. And that was for his sake, never mind Gabby's.

"I need my privacy!" Stella shouted.

"You can have all the privacy you want in the living room or out on the back deck!"

Stella began fulminating about rules and concentration camps and how her father took a bullet in Korea.

Very calmly, Harold intervened. In soothing, placating tones he said, "It's fine, Stell, it's fine. I've got my car. Let's go for a drive. It's a beautiful evening."

"I'm not going to see your mother."

"We'll go wherever you want."

* * *

After the couple left, Gabby was too hepped up to finish eating.

"Was that Grammy's boyfriend?"

"It looks that way."

"He said he loved her!"

"Yes. Very romantic."

"What's his name?"

"Harold Buckett."

"Harold *Buckett*?"

"Yes."

"That's weird … Did you know him before?"

"No."

"How old is he?"

"I don't know. Seventy, seventy-five."

"He eats a lot."

Or drinks, Oscar thought.

"Is he going to sleep over too?" Gabby said.

"No, bunny. No," Oscar said, frazzled, and thinking yet again that his mother had to go. As soon as possible.

But on that front, things weren't going so well. On Friday Oscar had called several area nursing homes, but had had no luck. They were either full up—the cheaper ones—or they had space but were too expensive. He still had other places to call, but more and more the reality of the situation was becoming clear: the easiest, and perhaps the only solution, was brother Duncan.

SEVEN

"Giddy-up, partner!"

This was Walter, with gleeful eyes and a comical grin, standing on Oscar's front porch. He had just rung the doorbell, and was wearing a ten-gallon hat and a red cowboy shirt with white fringe. Beneath this he wore cargo shorts and flip-flops.

"What's this, trick or treat?" Oscar said from the door, taking in Walter's duds and also the plastic shop bag he was holding.

They went up the stairs and into the living room. Stella was settled on the sofa, watching television.

"Hi Mrs. P."

Stella turned to the visitor. "Hello Walter ... You're looking trim."

Over the past few years Walter's waistline had noticeably swollen. Normally the one to do the ridiculing, he was now quiet, uncharacteristically mute. It reminded Oscar of when they were kids and Stella would razz the neighborhood boys and they would silently take it.

"What's with the getup?" she said.

"I'm helping out with the party."

"Oh yeah? Well go easy on the ponies—they're not pack mules."

Into the room came Gabby, eyes shining. "Uncle Walter!"

"Hey, it's the birthday girl! How are you, sweetie?"

"Gooood!" she said, drawing out the word with a big smile.

"Oh, that's good. Well, happy birthday. This is for you." He handed her the bag, then added, "I ran out of wrapping paper."

From the sofa, Stella snickered.

Gabby pulled a box out of the bag and stared at it. "Binoculars?"

"For when you and your dad go looking at birds and animals." One of Oscar and Gabby's pastimes was to walk local nature trails to observe wildlife. Gabby even kept a notebook in which she documented various sightings. "This way you'll see them better. See 'em up close."

"Oh, thank you!" the child said, now thrilled. She gave him a hug, wrapping her arms around his belly and bringing a bright smile to his face.

Again the doorbell rang, and over the next fifteen minutes it continued to ring as parents dropped off their little girls. Each of the kids came with a sleeping bag and a backpack filled with clothes and other essentials for the overnight shindig. Once they'd all arrived—Stacey Rumfola, Isabelle Yang, Yasmin Melendez, and Chloe Rakowitz—they deposited their stuff in the living room and prepared to head back out. The other three girls—Bonnie, Zora, and Sana—were driving with their parents straight to the farm. As they were leaving, Oscar told Stella they'd be back in a few hours; she had agreed to help with the pizza and movie later that evening.

"I'll be here," she said.

Out on the sidewalk Oscar said, "Who wants to ride with Walter?"

All the girls looked at him, the large man in the weird hat and shirt. There was a long silence. Then, just as it started to get awkward, Gabby said, "I will!"

Stacey and Chloe said they would ride with him too.

* * *

When the two-car convoy pulled into Lazy Bone Farm, there was only one car in the dirt parking lot: Duncan's candy-red Imperator sports sedan. Yet standing next to the car were both Duncan and Margot, along with their three girls—Bonnie to Duncan's right, and Zora and Sana well apart to Margot's left. They could have passed for a family.

Oscar parked beside the Imperator and there were greetings all around. To Margot he said, with a touch of concern, "You guys came together?"

She gave him a curious smile. "Yes."

Though it was just one small word—"Yes"—it had a big effect on Duncan: he seemed to grow several inches taller, his face radiant and proud.

Bonnie and the twins had run off to mingle with the other girls, and now Walter joined the adults. Oscar made the introduction.

"I love the hat," Margot said, grinning. "And the shirt. Now I feel underdressed."

"Well, I was worried Duncan was going to wear the same thing," Walter said. "But it looks like I'm OK."

Margot laughed; Duncan did not.

Walter said, "Hello Duncan. Great day for a ride, huh cowboy?" He held out his hand and they shook.

"Yeah. Great day," Duncan said, smirking with tolerant condescension.

With some exaggeration, Walter then zoned in on the Imperator, his eyes going round. "Whoa, that's quite the set of wheels. What is it, a 2019?"

Duncan said it was.

"What's she packing?"

"A V-12. Six hundred horsepower."

"*No*," Walter said, as if astounded.

"Yes," Duncan said earnestly. "You looking to buy?"

"Been thinking about it. What's the interior like? All leather?"

"Why don't we take a look," Duncan said, his tone and manner suddenly smooth and accommodating. He went around to the driver's side and opened the door. Walter followed.

Oscar knew exactly what Walter was up to, and he was grateful. Turning to Margot he said, "So how've you been?"

"Good. I have to say, the girls are very excited. They've been talking about this all week—the ponies *and* the sleepover. This will be our first night apart. I'm actually a little nervous."

"Oh, everything will be fine. These are great kids. And my mother's going to be with us tonight too. Helping out."

"I'm glad to hear that. And you have my number. In case anything happens."

"Yes."

Eyes warm with appreciation, Margot gave him another smile. Oscar held her gaze but she looked away.

"This place is so beautiful," she said, taking in the old farm-house and barn, the green pastures and the surrounding woods.

Oscar agreed, though he kept his eyes fixed on her: her thick dark hair, her elegant nose, her kissable mouth.

"I hope you don't mind," she said, now turning back to him, "but I looked you up online. I was curious to see your paintings."

"Really," he said, surprised.

"Yeah, I saw your website. I love your stuff. It's very alive. Lots of color, lots of light, lots of energy. There's a lot of feeling there. I can tell you love what you do."

Oscar was speechless. Blown away. Occasionally he met peo-ple who liked his work, and compliments were always nice. Par-ticularly if the person was interested in buying a painting. But this—from Margot—was like a gift.

"Now do you paint plein air?"

He was stunned, the woman surprising him yet again. "You know what plein air is?"

She laughed. "Yes. I told you I liked painting. And my ex collects art. Painting, sculpture, video. Though it's mainly con-temporary."

"I see … Uh, yes. I do paint plein air. As much as I can."

"Is that why you moved up here, to be closer to nature?"

"That was part of it."

"And why else?"

"Well, money for one thing. New York was just too expensive, and Lila, my wife, didn't want to raise Gabby in the city. She grew up in LA and wanted something a little slower paced. And she really loved Beauville."

"And what about you—do you love it here?"

"I do. Yeah."

"No regrets?"

"About leaving New York? No. Not at all. I miss my friends, and I miss the museums, but other than that, no. Do *you* have regrets?"

"Actually, no. The first couple of months were hard, but I'm liking it here more and more. I like the space, and the quiet. I think it's just what I needed, to tell you the truth."

At that moment, a middle-aged woman emerged from the farmhouse and the conversation stopped.

The woman was husky and unsmiling and walked with a limp. She came into the parking area, and once everyone had gathered around, she introduced herself as "Kat Pidgeon, proprietress of Lazy Bone Farm." The name, or the title, or the woman's stern businesslike manner, seemed to tickle Walter. A mirthful expression passed over his face, but he made no comment.

Oscar stepped forward and told Kat Pidgeon that they had spoken on the phone. He handed her an envelope filled with cash and she removed the bills and counted them very carefully. Then she counted them again. In silence, all the little girls watched. Satisfied with the transaction, the Proprietress, who had yet to address or even acknowledge the kids, led the entire party into the barn.

The first thing Oscar noticed was the smell. Others did too.

"Oh man," Duncan said, distorting his face and waving a hand in front of his nose.

"It stinks!" Bonnie said, now waving a hand in front of her nose.

Imperturbed, the Proprietress said, "This is a barn, not a candy shop."

But Gabby and the other girls seemed oblivious to the smell. For along one wall there were several horses in straw-filled stalls, and toward the back was a large pen for the ponies. Enthralled, the kids began murmuring and exclaiming "Ooooh!" "Wow!" "Look!" "Aaaawww!" Gabby herself appeared in heaven, her eyes rapt, entranced by all these precious creatures.

Then a voice shrieked, piercing every ear. With a mix of horror and rage, Bonnie cried out, "I stepped in doody!" She was wearing red-leather cowgirl boots, one of which was now partly brown. "Somebody clean it!" she screamed.

"*Bonnie!*" Duncan shouted.

But this did nothing; the kid was in hysterics, wildly flailing her arms. "*Somebody clean it!*" she demanded, stomping her foot.

In a huff, Duncan turned on the Proprietress. "You got a rag in this place?" His tone was insolent and belittling, making the request sound more like an insult.

Affronted, the Proprietress sniffed, "No, I do not have a *shit rag*. Take the kid outside and wipe her boot on the grass."

Walter tried, but mostly failed, to suppress a laugh. Two of the girls—Isabelle and Yasmin—caught this, and themselves began to giggle. Now seething, Duncan took Bonnie by the arm and led her back toward the entrance.

* * *

Minus two persons, the group proceeded into the pen—with everyone carefully watching their step. The ponies, docile yet aware, their eyes taking in the strangers, were already saddled up. The animals had stocky builds but luxurious manes and tails. Amid them stood a rail-thin, wizen-faced older man, mid-sixties, with a hard suspicious gaze.

"This is Brownie," the Proprietress said, indicating the man.

Brownie just nodded, then made a barely concealed sneer.

Turning to the girls, the Proprietress instructed them to go pet the ponies. There was some hesitation, but not from Gabby. She stepped up to the nearest one and began stroking its mane. Other girls followed and soon there was much cooing and sighing as they all realized how gentle and unthreatening the beasts actually were.

"OK," the Proprietress said, moving things along, "whose birthday is it?"

Somewhat shyly, Gabby raised a hand.

"You get to pick the first pony."

A tremor of excitement passed through the girls, and Gabby eagerly began looking from one animal to the next. Once she'd made her choice, the child stood beside her pony and began petting it. The Proprietress then gave the command for the rest of the girls to make their pick. All at once there was a flurry of activity, a scrambling of little bodies as though it were a game of musical chairs.

After all the selections had been made, Bonnie and Duncan rejoined the group. Coming into the pen with her freshly cleaned boot, Bonnie gave the Proprietress a murderous glare, her little eyes hungry for vengeance.

Smirking at this, the Proprietress said, "Just in time. Wild Thing's waiting for you."

"Wild Thing," evidently, was the name of the one pony none of the other girls had wanted. The name was clearly a joke. Or at least, Wild Thing had been nothing of the sort for a good ten, twenty years. The animal had a tired, elderly aspect—shrunken back, listless eyes, an overall dispirited attitude.

"I'm not riding that!" Bonnie said. "He's fat and ugly!"

"*Bonnie!*" Duncan said.

"I don't even want to ride a pony—it's stupid! I want to ride a horse!"

"You're not big enough for a horse," the Proprietress said.

"I don't care!"

Duncan, sighing wearily, looked to Oscar. Oscar turned to the Proprietress.

As if reading his mind, she said, "Brownie could lead the horse, and the girl could sit on it."

"OK," Oscar said.

"That's another fifty dollars," the Proprietress said.

Oscar cringed. Between the ponies and the pizza, he was already tapped, his wallet empty. He looked at Duncan, but Duncan looked away. Aware that everyone was watching, including Margot, he said, "Do you take credit cards?"

Walter interjected: "You know what, let me get this. I owe you money anyway."

It wasn't true; Walter didn't owe Oscar a cent. "No, I've got it," he said. "Thank you."

Then another young voice cried out: "I want to ride a horse too!"

Heads turned. The speaker was Stacey Rumfola. Staring at Oscar, the child gave him a bold, self-righteous pout.

With a cross look on her face, Margot stepped forward. She had heard enough. "You girls aren't big enough for a horse," she said firmly, glaring at Stacey. The child's self-righteous air instantly went flat. "The ponies are fine," Margot continued. "For *everyone*." This last was directed at Bonnie.

"Well I'm not riding *that* pony!" Bonnie said, pointing with disgust at Wild Thing.

"That's enough!" Duncan said. "You *will* ride that pony, and you'll like it!"

"No I won't!"

"Bonnie!"

"I won't, I won't, I won't!"

A voice said, "You can have my pony."

Everyone looked. It was Gabby.

There was a brief, uncertain silence, then Duncan said to Bonnie, "See? Isn't that nice of Gabby. You can have her pony—"

"*Hold on*," Oscar said with some feeling. "Gabby … are you sure? This is *your* birthday."

The child nodded. "I'm sure."

Everyone then looked at Bonnie. Frowning, the child spent several long moments deliberating the offer, then said, "OK." In her red cowgirl boots she walked over and took the reins from Gabby. Gabby went up to Wild Thing and, smiling at the old pony, petted his muzzle and whispered something into his ear.

* * *

After he gave a brief tutorial on how to ride and control the ponies, Brownie got the girls into their saddles and led them out of the barn and into the pasture. Then on foot he guided them single file off toward a trail in the woods. According to the Proprietress, who had already returned to the farmhouse, the mile-long "scenic trail" cut through virgin forest and passed alongside a pond and also a stream with a twenty-foot-high waterfall. Margot, ever the vigilant mother, had chosen to accompany the caravan on foot. Walter had too. Duncan, however, had said he would stay behind. "I've got nice shoes on," he explained. Oscar felt compelled to stay behind as well; there was something he wanted to discuss with Duncan, and he thought this an opportune moment to do it.

And so, as the pony train slowly disappeared into the woods, the brothers Perilloux sat at a picnic table in the shade of a giant oak. For twenty minutes Duncan made calls and sent text messages—and completely ignored Oscar. In response, Oscar gazed at the sky, the trees, the farmhouse, the barn—waiting on his brother. Then, losing his patience, he began to mock a mockingbird that had alighted in the tree, high overhead. Whistling deftly, and loud, Oscar matched the bird note for note.

Mockingbird: "fweet-fweet, fweet-fweet, fweet-fweet"

Oscar: "fweet-fweet, fweet-fweet, fweet-fweet"

Mockingbird: "wee-oh, wee-oh, wee-oh"

Oscar: "wee-oh, wee-oh, wee-oh"

Mockingbird: "fyoo-fyoo-fyoo, fyoo-fyoo-fyoo"

Oscar: "fyoo-fyoo-fyoo, fyoo-fyoo-fyoo"

It wasn't long before Duncan had grown thoroughly annoyed. He got off the phone, glaring at Oscar.

Oscar stopped whistling, and with a serene, contented expression, he took in the cloudless blue sky. "Beautiful day, huh?"

"That it is," Duncan said, now with a sly, knowing look. It was as though he could sense what was coming.

Not wanting to give his brother the satisfaction, Oscar decided to start with a different topic. He said, "Margot's a nice girl."

Duncan agreed.

"How'd you meet her?"

"I sold her a car. An SUV. Gave her a good deal, too."

"*You* sold her the car?" The sole proprietor of four prosperous dealerships, and the employer of numerous salespersons, Duncan often liked to boast how he hadn't worked the lot in many years.

"Yep. I was walking through the showroom, saw her, and told the salesman to scram," he said with the smuggest of grins. "I came out of retirement. Worked the old magic."

For Oscar, this was too much. "Lucky her," he said.

Duncan's eyes narrowed and he gave Oscar a sharp, chippy look. Just like that, he was ready for battle.

"No, I mean it," Oscar said, in a passably earnest tone. "She's lucky to have met you. She got a new car and … made a new friend."

Duncan mulled this, studying Oscar, and soon his expression relaxed. Then, in a confiding tone, he said, "Well … that's the problem."

"The problem?"

"I'm having trouble closing the deal … if you know what I mean."

Oscar had a sense of his brother's meaning, but he wanted to hear him spell it out. " 'Closing the deal'?"

"You know."

"Sex?"

"Ha. I wish. I haven't even kissed her yet."

Oscar had to restrain himself. His impulse was to pump his fist and cry out, "Yes!" Instead, with feigned surprise, he said, "*Really?*" It wasn't a question so much as a statement, as in, "Margot has refused to kiss *you*? How bizarre!"

With this sentiment, Duncan readily agreed. "Yeah," he said sadly. "I'm sure it has to do with her ex. The guy sounds like a real asshole. A VC guy. You know, money obsessed."

"Money obsessed," Oscar repeated.

"Yeah."

"Hmm."

"Apparently it was a nasty divorce. She hasn't said much about it, but reading between the lines, I think he'd been cheating on her. For a couple years. Now I think she's a little skittish. You know, not ready to jump into anything."

"Yes."

"Anyway, we're going out tonight—"

"You are?" Oscar said, stung.

"Yeah. It's our third date—"

"*Third?*" Oscar said, now shocked but also very pleased. He had assumed there had been more dates.

"Yeah … Why are you smiling?"

"Am I smiling?"

"Hey," Duncan said, on to another matter, "would you mind taking the kids back to your place after this? Bonnie and the twins?"

"Uh, no. Why? What are you guys doing?"

"Oh, and do me a favor," Duncan went on, disregarding the question. "Keep an eye on Bonnie and Zora tonight. There's some bad blood there."

"What do you mean?"

"Because of the softball game."

"Right. Bonnie threw an elbow," Oscar said, recalling the incident that had left one of the twins laid out on the ground crying.

"That's what Margot says," Duncan said doubtfully. "It didn't happen. Bonnie would never hurt anyone. It's just not in her. Yelling, screaming, throwing a temper tantrum, sure. But violence? No. Regardless, just keep an eye out. With Margot everything's light and easy unless it involves her girls, then—watch out. She's like a grizzly bear with her cubs."

"I understand," Oscar said.

"Where the hell are they, anyway?" Duncan said, looking across the pasture for the return of the party. "Did Bronley or whatever his name is take them off to Canada? The guy looked pretty sketchy to me."

Duncan took up his phone and began tapping. Evidently, their little chat was over.

"Hey, there is one other thing," Oscar said.

The knowing look returned to Duncan's face. "Let me guess: you're having trouble with Ma, and you want me to help."

Oscar shrugged.

"It's not going to happen, Oscar. I warned you there'd be problems, and you didn't listen."

"Look, I've called around to some places and—"

"No, I don't want to hear it. I already told you, I'm done with her. We all make our choices, little brother. You made yours, but things aren't going to plan, so now you want me to bail you out. But I'm not going to do it." He stood, tapped his phone again, raised it to the side of his head, and walked away.

EIGHT

That evening Oscar sat out on the back deck, alone, sipping a glass of Kentucky bourbon. He was feeling good, feeling like he was just about there, just about home free. Despite the rocky start, the pony ride had proved a big success. Gabby and all the girls had had fun, even Bonnie. Since then the pizza had been eaten, the cake cut, and the kids were now watching *The Little Mermaid*. In an hour or two, hopefully, they would all be asleep. Oscar's only remaining task would take place tomorrow morning: a pancake breakfast. Stella, possibly, was going to help out. Not that Oscar was counting on it. When he had returned home from Lazy Bone Farm, with eight hungry little girls in tow, Stella was nowhere to be found. She had cleared out. Had Oscar been surprised? Not a bit. Not at this point. Regardless, after the pancake breakfast, parents would be called to pick up their kids and Oscar would not have to think about birthdays again for another, oh, three-hundred-and-forty days.

Contented by the thought, he took another sip from his glass. Then, from within the house, there came an eruption of high-pitched screams, shrieks of mortal terror. Dropping the glass, Oscar sprang up and raced through the kitchen and into the living room.

Amid a frantic scene, as little girls screeched and scrambled for cover, Bonnie and one of Margot's twins—Oscar still couldn't tell which was which—were pummeling each other. Bonnie was yanking on a handful of the twin's hair while simultaneously trying to kick her. For her part, and despite her hair being pulled —which forced her head into a downward-facing position—the twin was wildly lashing out. Looking like some manic bongo player, with her arms moving in a piston-like blur, she again and again landed open-handed slaps to Bonnie's skull.

"Hey! Hey! Stop that!" Oscar shouted. He thrust himself between the girls and was immediately struck on the arm and chest by several of the twin's errant slaps. "Stop it!"

The action slackened, then ceased. Bonnie, however, still had a handful of the twin's hair.

"Bonnie, let go," Oscar said.

The twin echoed the sentiment. "*Let go!*" she screamed.

But Bonnie didn't let go—which led the twin's twin to step forward and bellow, "*Let go Bonnie!*"

As patiently as he could, Oscar said, "Bonnie—please."

The girl looked up at him, then relented, releasing her grip.

Once again in control of her own head, the twin straightened her posture. With pure venom she said, "You're a *jerk!*"

"Well you're a *loser!*" Bonnie retorted. "*And* I hate you!"

"*I hate you!*" the twin said.

"That's enough!" Oscar said.

"*You're* a loser!" the twin's twin said, somewhat belatedly, stepping closer and looking as though she herself was going to have a go at Bonnie.

Unthinkingly, Oscar said, "Zora, *no!*"

The girl looked up at him, furious. "I'm *Sana!*"

"Sorry."

Thinking it best to separate the combatants, Oscar took the twins into his room. Or rather, Stella's room. After he had shut the door he asked Zora, the one who had been in the brawl, if she was OK. She said yes, but then started to cry. "I want to go home," she said, as the tears spilled. At this, Sana also started to cry, and she also said she wanted to go home. Margot's two little ones, in a strange home among strange people, were terrified and weeping. Imagining the repercussions—Margot's maternal fury, Duncan's patronizing reproach—Oscar groaned and briefly shut his eyes, pained.

With a sigh he said, "OK. I call your mom. You'll be home soon ... And girls, I'm very sorry this happened. *Very* sorry. Gabby likes you both very much, all right? So don't be mad at her."

The twins nodded, in unison.

When Oscar reentered the living room Bonnie was talking on a pink cell phone. "I hate it here! I want to leave!" Then, to Oscar she said, "My dad wants to talk to you."

Wincing, Oscar took the phone.

"What the hell's going on over there, Oscar?" Duncan roared. "Bonnie and Zora are *fighting?*"

Oscar faltered. "Fighting's ... a strong word. It was ... more of a tussle."

"A *tussle?*"

"Yeah. A little hair-pulling, a couple slaps, then it was over. Everyone's fine."

"*Hair-pulling?* Look, we're coming over there now. Margot's with me. This is bullshit, Oscar! *Bullshit!*"

After he hung up and returned the phone to Bonnie, Oscar looked for Gabby. The child was seated on the sofa, eyes downcast, her expression dejected and forlorn. It was one of the saddest faces he had ever seen. His heart sank.

Turning to Bonnie he said, "Your dad's coming now. He'll take you home."

"*I want to go home too,*" said an incensed voice. It was Stacey Rumfola—the girl who, from earlier that day, had also wanted to ride a horse rather than a pony. Evidently, Bonnie was her role model.

Oscar looked at the other girls. "*Anyone else?*" It was said with a touch more feeling than he may have intended.

Despite their long faces, Isabelle, Chloe, and Yasmin shook their heads. Oscar told Gabby to take the girls to her room. The kids gathered up their sleeping bags and backpacks and followed their host down the hall.

Now alone with Bonnie and Stacey, Oscar asked Bonnie what caused the fight.

"I didn't want to watch that stupid movie. It's for little kids."

"I see," Oscar said, though in fact he didn't. But then, he was talking to an irascible eight year old. Hoping for a little more clarity he said, "You thought the movie was stupid, so you got mad at Zora."

"*Yes!*"

"OK," Oscar said, and he decided to leave it at that.

When the doorbell rang, he told Bonnie to wait where she was. "I'm going to talk to your dad and Mrs. Saadeh for a minute. Then you can come down."

Bonnie snarled at him, "You can't tell me what to do!" Grabbing her sleeping bag and backpack, she marched past him and went down the stairs to the front door. Stacey Rumfola followed, her chin raised high and her face glowing with righteous indignation.

Trailing the girls down the stairs, Oscar readied himself for trouble. And when he stepped onto the porch, he got it. Margot's incandescent glare withered him on the spot. Duncan was glaring too. Though he soon turned away, to escort Bonnie and Stacey down the porch steps and over to the Imperator.

"What happened?" Margot said.

"I don't know. Something about a movie."

"And where are my daughters?"

"They're upstairs. They're fine," Oscar said—but realizing this wasn't wholly accurate, he added, "Physically."

Margot tensed: first with confusion, then with growing fury.

Duncan came back up onto the porch. "What the hell, Oscar? I entrust my daughter to you, and now *this*?"

Oscar said nothing.

"So what happened?" Duncan demanded. "Bonnie says ..." He paused and glanced cautiously at Margot, then lowered his voice, speaking with amazed disbelief, "that Zora *hit* her?"

Margot shot Duncan an angry look.

"I don't know," Oscar said. "I don't know who started it."

With a great display of exasperation, Duncan waved a hand in Oscar's direction and said, to Margot, "He doesn't know … He doesn't know!" Then to Oscar he said, accusingly, "And so where were you when this happened?"

"Outside … On the deck."

"*Outside … On the deck*," Duncan repeated with acid sarcasm. Again he looked at Margot, now as if to say, "Can you believe this imbecile?" Continuing his interrogation, he said, "And were you drinking? Bonnie said she smelled booze on your breath."

Oscar looked away, incredulous—the little brat! Once he'd composed himself he said, "I had one drink. Actually, half of one drink. It's been a long day."

"*A long day*," Duncan said, mocking him. And then, shifting his tone from derision to straight-up indignation, he delivered his coup de grâce: "And didn't I tell you, Oscar—didn't I *specifically* tell you, not even three, four hours ago—to keep an eye on Bonnie and Zora? Didn't I do that?"

Oscar the human punching bag. He nodded. "Yes. You did." Penitent and ashamed, he lowered his eyes. Then he looked up —at Margot.

Throbbing with emotion, her eyes burning with wrath, she was clearly fighting to control herself, fighting to control her tongue. But at last the words came—sharp as a slap across the face: "What kind of a parent are you anyway?"

* * *

"Ouch," Walter said.

He and Oscar, naked but for the white towels around their waists, were sitting in the sauna at the Y, post-basketball. Oscar had just related the events of the birthday debacle: the Bonnie/Zora dustup, the collapse of the party, Duncan's theatrical tongue-lashing, and Margot's nuclear rebuke.

"She really gave it to you, huh?"

"Oh yeah. Both barrels."

Walter was grinning, and shaking his head. "Fricking Duncan. No offense but, he was always a bit of a crybaby. A tattletale. Remember that time back in middle school, and a bunch of us were throwing snowballs at cars? We were in the woods at Bennet Park?"

"Yeah. Some old lady pulled to the side of the road, backed up her car, and we all took off. Everyone except Duncan."

Walter laughed. "I couldn't believe it. He just stood there, and the lady gets out of the car and starts yelling at him. We're all hiding behind trees and watching, and she gets him to tell her his name and where he lives. Then he gives her everyone else's name too, the little bastard. By the time I got home the woman had already called Big Walter. I got a hell of a beating."

Oscar was smiling at the memory, but said nothing.

"So what happened afterward—after the 'What kind of a parent are you' slam?"

"Margot came up into the apartment, got her kids, and called an Uber. Duncan tried to talk her out of it. He said they could all ride together in his car, that the kids could make up. But Margot wasn't having it. By that point she seemed about as mad at him as she was at me."

"Have you talked to her since?"

"No."

"What about Duncan?"

"No. Neither of them."

"So what caused the fight? Did you ever find out?"

"According to Gabby, Bonnie got bored with the movie they were watching and said she wanted to watch something else. So to please her they stopped the movie and started going through Gabby's DVDs to find a better option. One of the twins saw the *Charlie Brown Christmas* special and said she wanted to watch that. But Bonnie apparently said it was 'stupid' and 'not winter' and also that Santa Claus 'isn't real,' at which point Sana started crying. She and her sister are younger than Bonnie. So Zora comes to her sister's defense, and there's a debate about Santa, if he's real or not, and the next thing you know Zora takes a swing at Bonnie and Bonnie grabs a handful of Zora's hair, and it was on. Little-girl MMA."

Walter was laughing. "I tell you … that Bonnie. She could use a good kick in the ass, huh?"

Oscar shrugged. "She's had a tough start. Her mother left her … and all the rest."

Walter nodded, then said, "And how's Gabby doing, the poor kid."

"She's OK. There were some problems with Bonnie, at school, but I think those have been worked out … Actually, she said something that's stuck with me. After Duncan and Margot left I sat her down to find out what caused the fight. And when she got to the part where Bonnie and the twins were debating if Santa was real, she said Bonnie got mad at her too. I asked why and she said, 'Because I said Santa was real.' I said, 'Why did you say that? You've known for a while now that Santa is make believe.' And she said, 'I know. But I didn't want Zora and Sana to be sad.'"

* * *

From the Y, Oscar and Walter walked over to the Brewhouse. They had just sat down in their usual booth when the manager came over. Oscar knew the guy was the manager because he wore a namepin that read, "Logan Stoltenham / Manager." He was young, mid-twenties, and possibly some sort of athlete—the tight-fitting jerseys he regularly wore gave full display of his toned chest and arms. Yet his rugged physique was undercut by his servile, fawning manner. For the past year or so, since he'd started the job, the guy had come to Oscar and Walter's table every Thursday night to interrupt their conversation and ask inane questions: "Gentlemen, welcome. Are you enjoying yourselves this evening?" Or, "And how are you finding the service tonight? Is it meeting your expectations?" Given the setting—the Brewhouse was a fairly dingy place, with sticky floors, greasy plastic menus, and graffiti-covered bathrooms—the questions and the guy's "professional" manner seemed frankly ludicrous.

Tonight, though, the manager's usual obsequious smile was absent. Instead his demeanor, though still "professional," was sober and firm. To Walter he said, as if addressing him for the first time, "Pardon me ... *Walter?*"

"Yeah. That's me."

"I'm sorry, Walter, but you're no longer welcome at the Brewhouse."

"Excuse me?"

"You're no longer welcome here. I'm afraid you have to leave."

"What the hell are you talking about?" Walter said, bewildered.

"I've had a report of sexual harassment made against you by one of my staff."

"*What?*"

"The incident occurred last Thursday evening."

"*Incident?*"

"Yes."

"And what exactly was this 'incident'?"

With arms clasped behind his back, Logan Stoltenham leaned forward at the waist and spoke in a discreet tone, as if to make his communication more confidential: "I'm under no legal obligation to tell you that information."

Walter, in a tone that *wasn't* discreet, said, "Kid, let me tell you something. I've been coming to this shithole for twenty years, since it first opened. You were probably still in kindergarten, eating your boogers and peeing your bed. If you're gonna kick me out after all these years, I want to know why."

The manager considered this. Still with the hushed voice he said, "You made a comment about one of the waitperson's ... anatomy."

"That's ridiculous ... Their 'anatomy'?"

"You said they had ... 'nice melons.' "

"I never said that!"

"That's what the waitperson said—and I believe her! I mean, *them*."

Fuming, Walter said, "Listen you little shit, what I said was, as I recall, 'I want something melon-y' … Now, was it suggestive? Perhaps. But I never said she had nice melons! I never said that."

"I'm sorry, but the waitperson—"

"And stop calling her 'the waitperson'! We all know her name is Pam—I know it, you know it, all the drunks at the bar know it!"

"*Sir*, please. The *waitperson* felt violated by the encounter. She said you demeaned her—"

"*I* demeaned *her*?"

"Yes. And whether the comment was direct or suggestive is irrelevant. At the Beauville Brewhouse, we are dedicated to providing a harassment-free work environment—"

"Oh shut up you pathetic eunuch!" Walter said, as he broke into a hearty laugh. "Fine … I'll go. You win." He slid his heavy frame out of the booth, then rose up to his full six-foot-three height, towering over the manager. He said, "Kid, enjoy your life. I have no doubt you'll go far … And the sad thing is, I mean it."

As Walter and Oscar passed through the restaurant toward the exit, they saw Pam herself. Standing behind the bar in one of her skin-baring blouses, she gave Walter a triumphant smirk, then casually flipped him the bird.

NINE

Ejected from the Brewhouse, Walter and Oscar decided to walk two blocks over to Froggie's Tap Room. As they went, each of them holding a gym bag, Walter grumbled and vented.

"I'm telling you, I don't understand these damn kids—these 'millennials.' Seriously, have you ever seen such sanctimony? Such piousness? Since when are *kids* so damn priggish and holier-than-thou? In our day, it was the *adults* who were the assholes! What the hell's wrong with them? A generation of pimply-faced Puritans: 'You can't say this, you can't say that.' What are they afraid of? And why are they so goddamn humorless? I've never seen anything like it. And where did it come from? School? The internet? Mothers Against Drunk Driving? Because it's not just words. These kids are boring as hell too. Even these kids we play hoops with, the ones on the Beauville varsity. I say to them, 'So how's the party scene, after the games?' Blank faces. All of them. It was the same with Walter the third. He made varsity football his sophomore year, and after his first game, Friday night under the lights, he came straight home after it was over. I said, 'What are you doing? Why aren't you at the party?' He said, 'What party?' I said, 'Isn't there a football party tonight?' He had no idea what I was talking about. When we were kids, half the reason you *even played* football was for the parties! You played the games, then you went out and got shit-faced with your buddies. You drank, you flirted with the girls, and maybe you got lucky. But not these kids! *Noooo!* These kids are home at night, playing video games and posting pictures of themselves on Facebook! I just don't understand it. They spend half their damn lives looking at their phones! Seriously, that's what they do. It's pathetic and embarrassing. They should be out with their friends, raising hell. And OK, sure—there were some casualties back in the day, back when we were kids. I'll admit it. Some drunk driving fatalities. Those two cheerleaders junior year, and then what's-his-name, the hockey player. And Ronnie Trout getting tanked and passing out in the woods that winter and then having to get his foot amputated. And Jakey Nolan getting brain damage after he took LSD and fell out of that tree. Sure. Unfortunate stuff. But we had fun, Oscar—remember? We lived! We really did. Those were great days."

* * *

Inside Froggie's—which had been a local dive even when Oscar was a kid—things were on the quiet side. Whereas the Brewhouse had continuous piped-in "classic rock" and a dozen or so TVs tuned to sports and news channels, Froggie's had just one TV and no music. The TV sat behind the bar and was now showing a Red Sox game. There were maybe ten people in the place, including three solitary drinkers at the bar.

Oscar and Walter took a booth and soon a waitress came over. She was older than Oscar and had a 1980s haircut, one that must have required lots of hairspray.

She said, "Hey Walter."

"Hey Heidi. How are ya?"

They chatted for a bit, then Walter asked for a couple menus.

* * *

Over their second round of beers, Walter said, "I have a question for you."

"OK," Oscar said.

"Why do you go to church?"

Ever so slightly, Oscar flinched. Religion wasn't one of Walter's usual barroom topics. "Why do you ask?"

"I don't know. Is it for Gabby? So she gets some sort of, what, moral grounding?"

"That's part of it."

"What's the other part?"

"The other part is that I believe."

"You believe in God."

"Yes."

Walter pondered this, then sipped his beer. "And when did that start? I just remember in high school you weren't exactly the religious type." There was a mischievous glint in his eye, as he was no doubt recalling their youthful debauches.

"That's true," Oscar smiled. "Though I'm not sure there is a religious 'type.' For me it started when I was a kid. Duncan and I were raised Catholic—Sunday school, first communion, the whole thing. But after my father died my mother stopped taking us."

"She lost her faith?"

"No. I think it was my dad who was the religious one. She just went along with it."

"When did you start going again?"

"Well … it was after Lila got her first diagnosis. On our wedding trip she found a lump on her neck and when we got back we learned it was cancer. She was pretty devastated, and eventually she started going."

"She was Catholic too?"

"Yes. Lapsed."

"OK … That makes sense. But what about the pedophiles?"

Oscar cringed. "The pedophiles?"

"Yeah, you know … I guess I don't understand why you or anyone would want to be associated with that."

Oscar paused, looking at Walter. Then he nodded and briefly lowered his eyes. "Yes … It is a stumbling block. And for the record, I'm probably more sickened by it than you are."

"Then why do you stay?"

"I stay because I believe. When Lila first started going I was basically an agnostic, but I went with her to be supportive. She thought she was going to die and I didn't want her to feel alone. And then after she got through it, after the cancer went away, she said she wanted a baby. For me that was just as much of a shock as her getting sick. When we first met, and all the way through to when we were married, she showed no interest in having kids. She used to say, 'My students are enough.' But that all changed. She wanted to have a family, and when Gabby came, she wanted to raise her in the faith. So now church was a regular thing.

"I don't know when it happened exactly, but at some point I also started to believe. I realized I was getting something out of the Mass, that I wasn't going just to be a 'supportive husband.' Life was starting to make sense. But then something unexpected happened. Not long after I started to believe, Lila's cancer returned. And I remember as soon as I learned the news—we were living in Beauville at that point—I became furious. Really, really furious. At God, at Jesus. I had thought that if you were 'good,' if you believed and went to church and all the rest, that somehow He would take care of things, that bad things wouldn't happen to you ..." Oscar chuckled. "Obviously, that's very naive. But that's what happened. I was mad and I didn't want to go to church anymore. But Lila, she felt just the opposite. With the second diagnosis she basically doubled down. She started praying more and going to Mass during the week. And all the while she stayed strong, stayed in good spirits. I was more depressed, and more afraid, and more angry, than she was. It didn't seem fair, her getting sick again. But she kept fighting, and smiling, and telling me she had complete trust in God. And in the last few months, when she was in bed all the time, it was the same. She never lost her faith. I asked her why and she said, 'I couldn't imagine going through this *without* faith; God is here for me; I'm not alone.' It was at that point that I started to get it."

"What?"

"That the more you trust in God, the more you reach out to Him, the more He's with you. It's hard to explain, but it's essentially what the Church means by 'grace.' It's an experience that devout people have, where they feel God's presence, where they don't feel alone, where they feel hope and peace and even sometimes joy. I think Lila experienced this. In fact, I'm sure she did."

"Have you?"

"Me?"

"Yeah."

Oscar shrugged. "I think ... I think I've had little tastes of it. Enough to know I'm on the right path."

Walter contemplated this, and drank from his beer. "In my family, we were Lutheran. My parents brought my sisters and me to church until, I don't know, junior high. Then it just kind of fizzled. I don't know why ... But the thing is, I'm just not sure I buy it."

"What?"

"God, Jesus. Rising from the dead, the afterlife ... It just seems ... I don't know. What about Buddhism?"

"Buddhism?"

"Yeah. It's like a religion without the guilt, right?"

"Uh, well ..."

"Do you know anything about it? Have you read anything?"

"A little. After college I read some of the foundational texts —the *Dhammapada*, the Four Noble Truths. And also stuff by different monks and lamas. Some of my friends in New York are Buddhists."

Walter grew silent, then said, "I ask because ... I need *something*." And all at once there was a look on his face that Oscar had never seen before: desperate, anguished, vulnerable. A look of suffering. "My life's in the toilet, Oscar. It's just floating there like some turd, and everyone around me seems more than happy to flush it away. Carole left me. My kids ignore me. I'm getting old, I'm getting fat. I drink too much. I think I'm addicted to porn. This is not the life I expected."

These were startling revelations. Previously, Walter had spoken of his unhappiness in more general terms: he missed married life, he missed his kids, he missed his father. Et cetera. Never before had he spoken this candidly.

And he wasn't finished. "About a year ago I went to see a shrink. I'd started wondering if I wanted to live anymore. I kept asking myself, What's the point of it all? *What's the damn point?* I had no answer. So halfway through the first session the guy says I'm depressed and that it's very common and he's going to prescribe some pills. Pacifil. And so I say, 'Fine. I'll take anything. I don't want to feel like this.' So I get the pills, but before I took one I wanted to make sure I knew what I was doing. I googled Pacifil, and the first hit I get is that it can cause all sorts of side effects: insomnia, weight gain, impotence, suicidal ideation. And I'm thinking, Weight gain? Impotence? Suicidal ideation? I'm already 'ideating' suicide as it is, so how the hell is this supposed to help? If anything, it's probably going to push me over the edge. Then I read another article that said antidepressants are no more effective than exercise or placebo. *What?* A fake pill works as much as the real one? What's going on here? Then I read another article that said forty million Americans take these things. *Forty million!* Think about that. Forty million people are so unhappy with life that they feel the need to take a pill that alters their brain chemistry and gives them all sorts of side effects— including a limp dick, should they have one. What does that say about this country?"

"That's a good question," Oscar said.

Walter tipped back his beer, then went silent.

The silence lengthened, until Oscar said, "So what happened?"

"What do you mean?"

"Did you take the pills?"

Walter glanced away, looking uneasy. "Yeah."

"Have they helped?"

"I don't know. I can't tell. Some days I think so, and others I don't."

"And what about the therapy? Is that helping?"

"Eh ... so-so. I see the guy once a month. To be honest, I don't really think about dying anymore, so maybe it is helping."

"That's good."

"Yeah. But I still have the same question: what's the point of it all?"

"What are your thoughts?"

"I don't know. That's the problem. I just don't know." He shook his head. "Maybe I just need a woman."

"What does your shrink say?"

"He says I should get a dog."

* * *

When Oscar returned home, he found Stella, Gabby, and Mackenzie the babysitter all sitting on the sofa. On the coffee table was an empty half-gallon carton of pistachio ice cream and three empty bowls with spoons. And on the television, which filled the room with applause and a pulsing Latin beat, a very energetic couple dipped and twirled across the dancefloor.

Unlike last week, when Oscar's arrival had sent Gabby into a guilty panic, tonight she met him with an ecstatic smile. "Hi Daddy!"

Following the birthday disaster, Oscar had asked the child how they could make up for it. Was there anything special she wanted to do? Gabby gave the question her full attention. Then, with a cautious but hopeful air, she'd said, "Can I watch the dancing show with Grammy again?" After a moment's reflection Oscar said, "Sure." Thrilled by this great windfall, the child decided to roll the dice yet again: "And can we have ice cream too?" Oscar said, "I think that would be fine."

Now he said, "How are you bunny?"

"Gooood! We're watching the dancing show."

"Yes. I can see that."

This got a giggle from Mackenzie. She was a freshman at Beauville High and lived two doors down. She had acne, curly red hair, and a very cheery demeanor. For whatever reason, she giggled whenever Oscar spoke to her.

"Everything go OK tonight?" he said, addressing her now.

"Yeah," the girl said, then giggled.

"Gabby had her bath?"

Another giggle. "Yeah, right before this started," she said, glancing at the TV. "Is it OK if I finish watching this?"

"Oh—of course," Oscar said. "Sorry to interrupt."

Again Mackenzie giggled. "That's OK." She turned her eyes back to the screen and instantly became as engrossed in the action as Gabby and Stella.

* * *

After the show had ended, and Mackenzie departed with a final giggle, Oscar told Gabby it was time for bed. Still seated on the sofa, the child turned to Stella and embraced her in a sudden, impulsive hug. Wrapping both hands around her grandmother's neck she said, "Good night Grammy!"

Startled by this burst of affection, Stella went very stiff. Her eyes flashed with confusion and worry. Maybe even fear. But she wasn't the only one: Oscar was horrified. This wasn't something he wanted to see—his daughter forming an attachment to his mother. It wasn't a good idea. In addition to the drinking and the vaping and the constant television-watching, there had been Gabby's birthday. Not only had Stella skipped out on the party to spend the evening instead with Harold at Sligo's Saloon, smoking cigarettes and drinking gin, she hadn't even bothered to get her granddaughter a gift or even a card. Not that Gabby seemed to care. She hadn't even mentioned it. Regardless, Oscar knew the child was likely craving maternal affection. She'd been without a mother now for three years. Surely some part of her was longing for a loving female presence. But in Oscar's mind there could be no worse candidate for the role than Stella Perilloux.

He said, "Come on Gabby, let's go. You have school tomorrow, and Grammy and I have a big day too. I'm taking her to look at a new place to live."

"You are?" the child said, her little face suddenly filled with distress.

"Yes," Oscar said, and it was true. One of the old folks' homes he had phoned the previous week had called back earlier that day to say they now had an "available bed."

With sad questioning eyes Gabby turned to Stella, "Don't you want to live with us anymore?"

Before Stella could respond Oscar said, "Grammy is just living here temporarily. I told you that already. A few times, remember?"

The child made no reply, nor did she look at Oscar. Instead she continued to look expectantly at Stella, while Stella, looking back at the child, said nothing.

"Gabby, come on," Oscar said. "Let's go."

* * *

Late the next morning Oscar and Stella pulled into the parking lot at Riverside Pines Retirement Home, up on the Beauville Heights. It was a large, gloomy-looking building of painted stucco. There were cracks in the exterior walls and patches of black mold. On one side of the building was a gas station; on the other, a funeral home.

Inside, the lobby was deserted. At the front desk was a hand-written note that read, "Back in five." Oscar and Stella waited. Five minutes passed, then ten. Oscar went over to the directory by the elevator. The administrative offices were one flight up.

When they stepped off the elevator, Oscar just stared. In what evidently was a public lounge, fifteen or so elderly people were gathered around a single television. Some sat on easy chairs, others on sofas, and still others in wheelchairs. Half of them seemed to be sleeping. Or at least, Oscar hoped they were sleeping. Their heads were either bowed over, chins resting on their chests, or else craned back, chins pointing up at the ceiling, mouths gaping and eyes shut. Those not sleeping were focused on the TV, watching as a middle-aged man excitedly tried to guess the price of a new washing machine while the studio audience wildly cheered him on. But no one here was cheering. Apart from the television, the large space was eerily silent.

The scene unsettled Oscar. Stella too.

"They're all old!" she said.

Looking for signs of life, Oscar spotted a nurses' station at the far side of the room. "Ma, come on."

The nurses' station was set behind a long counter topped by a wall of plexiglass with a single small opening, like a bank teller's window. Oscar stepped up to the opening.

Behind the glass and off to the side, ten feet away, three women in pink scrubs stood chatting. One of the women glanced over at Oscar, then promptly resumed the conversation with her colleagues. A couple minutes passed. The woman glanced back at Oscar, made an irritated face, and walked up to him.

"I'm looking for Marnie Kepple," he said.

"You need to go down to the front desk," the nurse said brusquely, then turned to rejoin her friends.

"There's no one there," Oscar said.

The nurse rolled her eyes, then reached for a phone. Ten minutes later a woman with an ebullient air bounded into the room. She came right over to Oscar and Stella.

"You must be the Perillouxs!" she said joyously, as if this was one of the great moments of her life.

"That's right," Oscar said.

"And you must be Ollie," Marnie Kepple said, extending a hand.

"Oscar," he said, shaking her hand.

"What?"

"My name is Oscar. Not Ollie."

"*Oh!* Right, right—*Oscar.* We talked yesterday. How could I forget?" The woman laughed with mock-disbelief, as if the joke was on her. Turning to Stella, she tilted her head to one side and gazed with soft, caring eyes. In a syrupy voice, a voice used with a child, she said, "And you must be Stella ... How are you sweetie?"

With the oxygen tubes affixed to her nostrils, Stella gave Marnie Kepple a blunt stare, saying, "Lady, let's get one thing straight. I'm not your sweetie."

Marnie Kepple perked up, energized, as if thrilled by this un-expected retort. To Oscar she said, "*Ohhh*, she's feisty! This is going to be *fun*! ... Why don't we take a tour of the facility."

With Marnie leading the way, they went down a long cor-ridor to the assisted-living wing. First they saw what Marnie described as "the rec room," an airy, windowless space in which a number of seniors were being led through a square-dance session. A fiddle-heavy tune played from a boom box while a bored-look-ing twentysomething called out instructions to the slow-moving dancers. Some had uninterested expressions, others smiled with imbecilic glee.

"This might be fun for you, Stella," Marnie said, "but your air tank might make things difficult. We did have an unfortunate accident last year."

Next they went to what Marnie called "the dining room"—which in fact was a cafeteria. The place was empty except for a lanky teenager in white kitchen clothes who was staring intently at his phone. Marnie offered her guests a "complimentary beverage," but Oscar and Stella declined. After this they went to "the fitness center"—a small, closet-sized room with a single stationary bike and a handful of two- and five-pound dumbbells. This space also was empty. And finally the trio stepped outside to "the garden"—a patch of weedy grass behind the building with two metal picnic tables, a couple tall pines, and a handful of marigolds and petunias in desperate need of water.

After taking in the trees and the flowers, Oscar said, "Where's the river?"

"The what?"

"The river … *Riverside* Pines?"

Marnie Kepple looked at him as if he was being difficult. "It's just a name," she said.

Oscar nodded. "I see."

At last the tour made its way to what would be Stella's living quarters: a small bedroom with a private bathroom. The walls were made of painted cinderblocks and the room's two windows looked out onto Blutowski's Funeral Home and Crematorium. Yet more noticeable than the small space and the depressing view was the pronounced, nose-wrinkling scent of urine.

"Well Stella, how do you like your new home?" Marnie said, flashing a smile that would have made a flight attendant proud.

"It smells like the toilets at Sligo's Saloon."

Bewildered, Marnie gave the air two dainty sniffs. "I think that's just disinfectant."

"No. It's piss," Oscar corrected her.

"Well I know for a fact," Marnie said, with a stiff smile and straining patience, "that our excellent housekeeping staff has given this room a thorough cleaning. But if it would make you happy, I will ask them to give it another round before your mother moves in."

"Do you have anything else?" Oscar said. "Another room?"

"I'm afraid not," Marnie said, now with a syrupy, go-to-hell smile. "I expect that I'll soon have a single suite available, with a kitchenette and full views of the garden—as poor Mr. Gallavedis isn't doing so well—but unfortunately that accommodation is substantially outside of Stella's affordability. As we discussed on the phone yesterday, Mr. Perilloux, your mother's options are very limited, based on her Social Security income and the amount that Medicare is willing to contribute. Given that situation, this really is the best I can do."

TEN

"Go kick some butt, OK?"

"OK!"

In her Vinny's Lube and Oil Change uniform, Gabby beamed and ran off with two of her friends.

Father and daughter had just arrived at Perilloux Field for another softball game. Oscar placed his helmet in the motorcycle's sidecar and started for the bleachers, his mood suddenly growing tense. He was expecting to see Duncan for the first time since the birthday party and was fairly certain there was going to be trouble. From childhood on Duncan had been a grudge-holder, a champion grievance-keeper—just like their mother. Also, Vinny's Lube and Oil Change were once again playing Lucky Garden, which meant Oscar might also be seeing Margot for the first time since the birthday party. In the two previous Sundays since then, Margot and her brood had not been at church.

But Margot wasn't in the bleachers. Instead Duncan was sitting by himself, five rows up. Oscar ascended the steps, and when Duncan saw him coming he made a petulant face, crossed his arms, and gazed out at the kids on the field.

"Mind if I sit here?" Oscar said.

"Go ahead," Duncan said, still looking at the field. "I paid for these bleachers. You might as well enjoy them."

Oscar felt the irritation rising, but he refrained from making a wisecrack. It required some effort. He sat on the plank beside his brother, and for a minute or two they were silent, each of them scowling as they watched the two teams going through their warm-ups. Oscar scanned the Lucky Garden side for Zora and Sana, but they weren't there.

At last he said, "So how've you been?"

"Me?" Duncan snarled. "Oh, I've been great. Just great. Except that Margot dumped me!"

" 'Dumped you'?"

"Yeah. After the birthday party. That's on you, Oscar!"

"Oh come on."

"What do you mean, 'Oh come on'?"

"You guys had what, three dates? What was there to dump?"

"Well if not for you, there would have been a fourth date, and then a fifth, and then a sixth."

"I see. If not for me, you probably would have married her, is that it?"

Duncan's face turned ugly. "You know Oscar, one of these days you're going to push me too far. I have my limits!"

There was more silence, and more scowling.

Finally Oscar said, "Look, I'm sorry, OK? I apologize. And I'm sorry about what happened with Margot. That was ... unfortunate."

Grudgingly, Duncan's expression softened. The strain and the animosity vanished, and soon were replaced by a look of suffering, a look of pain. "I'm telling you Oscar, I have strong feelings for that woman. I'm having trouble sleeping. She's all I can think about."

Oscar sighed. "When was the last time you talked to her?"

"The night of the party. At your house. We've exchanged a couple texts, but that's it."

"Well, maybe you'll see her today."

"No, she's not coming."

"Why?"

"She's in France. Her cousin's getting married, or got married. She left last week and is going to be away for a while. Two, maybe three weeks."

To Oscar, this was great news. Margot's trip to Europe meant that her absence from church, at least for the most recent Sunday, was not about her wanting to avoid him—something he had secretly feared. So that was good. *Very* good. But there was some bad news here as well. For despite everything, Oscar realized that his feelings for Margot Saadeh were as strong as ever. Just like brother Duncan's.

* * *

After the warm-ups, Vinny's Lube and Oil Change took the field to start the game. Oscar's paternal gaze followed his daughter as she ran out to left field. Once Gabby had assumed her position, Oscar focused on his niece at third base.

Following the great Santa Claus debate, which resulted in Bonnie grabbing a handful of Zora Saadeh's hair and Zora unleashing a barrage of roundhouse slaps, Bonnie had refused to speak to Gabby for having sided with the twins. This had gone on for several days at school, and had also included Stacey Rumfola and some of Bonnie's other friends. To this little-girl clique, formerly all Gabby's friends too, Gabby had become an elementary-school pariah—avoided in the classroom, shunned in the lunch room, mocked on the playground. Never before had the child experienced such treatment. For three days in a row she returned home in tears.

At this, Oscar had been livid, seething with fury at his niece and the rest of the grade-school she-bullies. But he'd not wanted Gabby to see his anger, so he kept it in check. Stella, however, had been less discreet. "That snot-nosed little bitch!" she'd cried, railing about Bonnie. "Give me five minutes with her and that'll be the end of it!" Several times Oscar had nearly picked up the phone to call his brother. But in the end he knew that Duncan would just get defensive and start yelling, which in turn would cause *him* to get defensive and start yelling, and the whole thing would become worse than it already was.

So Oscar decided to wait. To be patient. To give it a few days to see if things might calm down. In the meantime he did his best to comfort and reason with Gabby. He told her that sometimes people were mean, and that sometimes life wasn't fair. And he reminded her that Bonnie was family, and that family was one of life's most important things. (It seemed like the right thing to say.) And he predicted that soon this conflict would end, and eventually he was right. On the previous Thursday afternoon Gabby had returned home from school in good spirits. Bonnie had been "nice" to her and she was back to eating lunch with the girls and playing with them at recess. All, apparently, had been forgiven. Even so, Oscar had begun thinking it might not be a bad idea if Gabby were to make some new friends. Friends like Zora and Sana, for example.

Still watching his niece, Oscar said, "So how's Bonnie?"

"Bonnie?" Duncan said.

"Yeah."

"She's … OK. She's between nannies at the moment. That's why I'm here."

"Oh."

"Yeah, for some reason I'm having trouble finding a replacement for the one that left last month. Now I'm thinking I might hire a girl from overseas. Sweden, maybe. That way, she might be less likely to leave, you know?"

"I suppose."

"To tell you the truth," Duncan said in a lowered voice, not wanting any of the nearby parents to hear, "I'm kind of concerned about her."

"What do you mean?"

"Well … her psychiatrist wants her to start taking antidepressants."

"Her *psychiatrist*?"

"*Yes*. And keep your voice down."

"Sorry … How long has that been going on?"

"A couple years. She has ADHD—the attention deficit thing. She's been on Ritalin but that hasn't been working so now the woman thinks she has depression too. It appears there are some issues around her mother. It's why she acts up sometimes."

"Her mother," Oscar said.

"Yeah."

"OK. But is it safe? All these drugs? She's eight years old."

"She'll be nine in September. And yes, the psychiatrist says it's perfectly safe. And she should know, I'm paying her enough. Five hundred bucks an hour! But it's fine. She's one of the best shrinks in the state. An expert in the field. Harvard-trained and all the rest. Basically what it comes down to is, Bonnie has a chemical imbalance. That's really the heart of it. It's a genetic thing, something she was born with."

"I thought you said it had to do with her mother."

"It's not that simple, Oscar. Human psychology is very complex. Trust me, I deal with people all day long, all sorts of characters. As for Bonnie, yes, her mother has something to do with her problems. The way she abandoned her and everything else. But the main thing is the chemical imbalance—it leads to mood swings, which in turn leads to the behavior. The pills will address this. In a couple months, Bonnie will be fine."

* * *

Midway through the second inning there came a burst of carnivalesque music. It was the ice cream truck, "Mr. Sweety Sweets," pulling into the parking lot. All the girls on the field turned to look. The umpire did too. Kids not in uniform either ran to their parents to get money or went straight for the truck. Adults in the bleachers began to stir.

"Hey, you want an ice cream?" Duncan said.

"No, I'm fine," Oscar said.

"What about a hotdog?"

Oscar considered this. "OK. I'll take a hotdog."

Duncan reached for his wallet, then held out a fifty. "Get me a foot-long with relish and ketchup, and one of those strawberry shortcake ice creams—you know, the ones with the sprinkles."

Oscar stared at his brother. It was like when they were kids: Duncan presuming he was the boss and trying to order Oscar around. Then as now, the arrogance and the presumption of it deeply pissed him off. He said, "Actually, I think I'll pass."

Duncan made his annoyed face, eyes glaring, nostrils flaring. He looked over at the ice cream truck and vacillated. Then, in a huff, he stood and started down the bleachers.

When his brother got to the bottom rung, Oscar called out: "Hey Duncan."

Duncan looked back.

"Yeah, I'll take a hotdog," Oscar said. "Mustard and onions. And get me a Dr. Pepper too."

* * *

Chewing on the first bite of his hotdog, Duncan said, "So how's it going with Ma?" There was a gleeful glimmer in his eye, and it was hard to miss.

"OK," Oscar said, sipping his Dr. Pepper. "They offered her a spot at Riverside Pines."

"That place is a dump."

"I know."

Duncan swallowed, then said, "At least she's off your hands." He took another bite, watching the game.

"Actually, she's not."

"What do you mean?" Duncan said, turning on Oscar.

"We decided against it."

"*We?* Why?"

"It's like you said, the place is a dump. I wouldn't want to live there. The room smelled like piss."

"So then what are you going to do?"

"Keep looking."

"She's still at your place?"

"Yeah. Where else is she going to go?"

"Unbelievable," Duncan muttered, angrily shaking his head.

"What?"

"You take her into your home because you say you're trying to help her find a place. Then you find her a place, probably the best one she can afford, but that's not good enough for you."

"What do you care?" Oscar said, baffled. "This has nothing to do with you."

Duncan snapped: "To hell it doesn't! You're trying to make me look like the asshole—"

"*What?*"

"For twenty years I cleaned up after her and you did nothing. Absolutely nothing. From college on you just disappeared, pretended we didn't exist. But for whatever reason you decided to move back here and now you're trying to play the good son and make me look like the bad one. It pisses me off, Oscar! It pisses me off!"

"Duncan, do you know what a narcissist is?"

"Don't get smart with me Oscar!"

People were watching, and had been watching. But Duncan only noticed it now. He shut up.

As if by providence, Gabby cried out from left field: "*Daddy, look!*" The child pointed to the sky. Everyone in the bleachers redirected their eyes, craning their heads upward.

A little higher than a tall pine tree, seven hawks were flying in the same general direction. It was a fairly unusual sight. Thanks to *The Wild Life with Jamie and Gina*, Oscar knew that hawks mostly flew solo. He called back to his daughter: "Yeah, I see. That's great … Now pay attention to the game."

"*All right!*" the child shouted in a cheerful voice, then turned her eyes to the pitcher and batter.

From three rows beneath Oscar and Duncan, two women who just moments before had been watching the argument, now turned back with delighted smiles.

"Gabby is *so* cute!" one of them said.

"Adorable!" the other one said.

Somewhat awkwardly, Oscar returned the smiles. "Thanks."

The moment soon passed, and once again everyone was watching the action on the field rather than the action between the brothers Perilloux. For his part, Duncan had mostly calmed down. In peevish silence he finished the rest of his hotdog then started in on his strawberry shortcake ice cream, and for the rest of the game the subject of their mother was not mentioned.

* * *

Late the next afternoon, around five, Oscar caught a whiff of a tantalizing scent. It was warm and sweet, like the smell of a baking cake. Immediately he felt hungry, his mouth watering and his stomach demanding some attention.

He was up in his studio, seated before his easel. For some time he had been scrutinizing his latest work-in-progress, a landscape of an abandoned granite quarry. The previous two days he had lugged the canvas and his French easel a mile into the woods and up a hill to the water-filled quarry, which he, Duncan, and Walter had swam in as kids. Now, as he inspected the canvas, Oscar was assessing its progress. It was something he regularly did: sit in silence, staring at the work as it developed, session by session. His attention fully engaged, he would observe the color, the drawing, the composition—the painting's primary components —and analyze what was working and what wasn't. In this way, some deep part of his mind, his being, was activated, and it would instruct him on what to do next. It was uncanny to him, how the answers just came. Same too with the execution of the work. For occasionally, after a session in the studio or outside, in plein air, Oscar would be amazed by what he saw on his canvas—amazed because what he was looking at seemed beyond his capabilities. How had he possibly done that? How had he possibly created something this right, this beautiful? It was like a blessing, a gift. Was it always like that? No. Often there were periods of frustration and even despair—periods when he wondered if maybe he should have gone to law school. But always Oscar persisted and, eventually, the breakthrough would come. The moment when everything came together. The moment when brush and paint accomplished something magical. These were the moments of euphoria, the moments when all of his struggles and sacrifices and hard work paid off. The pleasure of it was almost beyond compare.

At this moment, however, with the warm sugary scent wafting into the studio, Oscar was thinking of another type of pleasure. Rising from his chair he followed the aroma down the stairs and into the kitchen. There he saw an astonishing sight: Stella standing by the stove and Gabby seated at the table, using her fingers to lick up the last bits of batter from a mixing bowl.

Looking extremely pleased, the child said, "Daddy, Grammy and me made blueberry muffins and they're gonna be really yummy!" The smile on her face could have lit up all of Beauville. All of New Hampshire.

Perplexed, and also vaguely suspicious—or maybe *keenly* suspicious—Oscar looked at his mother. Standing just feet away she met his eye with a cheery, sphinxlike gaze. Was it a look of wry amusement, Oscar wondered—or sly calculation?

"They're almost ready," she said.

And just then the timer began beeping. In a burst of excitement, Gabby clapped her hands, shot up from the chair, and sprang to the stove.

Like a seasoned chef, Stella took charge: "OK, watch out! This stove is hot. Where are the potholders?"

From one of the cabinet drawers Gabby got the potholders and handed them over. Stella opened the oven door and extracted two trays, each with six fragrant muffins.

"Can we have one now?" Gabby said.

"Nope. Your dad's gonna be cooking soon. We can have one for dessert."

Oscar, with a skeptical crease in his brow, noticed the box of Betty Crocker muffin mix on the counter. "Where did you get the mix? And the muffin trays?"

"Harold took me to DeSanti's yesterday," Stella said. "When you were at the softball game."

"This was your idea?"

"It was."

As far as Oscar knew, his mother had never baked a muffin in her life. Certainly she'd never done any baking when he and Duncan were kids. Occasionally, after her shift at the supermarket, she might bring home a box of Ring Dings or Whoopie Pies. But to actually *make* something herself? Muffins or cookies or cakes? No, that was what other moms did.

Clearly, something was up. Some scheme, some plot. And glancing down at Gabby's innocent joyful face, Oscar had a growing sense of what that might be. To his mother he said, "A new hobby, huh?"

Unfazed, Stella said, "That's right. It's never too late to start."

* * *

That night in Gabby's room, Oscar smiled at his daughter and said, "Ready?" He and the child were kneeling at the foot of her bed, facing the icon of Mary and baby Jesus that hung on the wall, above the headboard. Smiling back at her father, Gabby nodded, and together they made the sign of the cross.

In the years before she died, Lila had devised Gabby's nightly routine: piano, bath, prayers, story time, lights out. And she'd been the one to oversee the various activities. Not because Oscar hadn't offered to help—he had—but because Lila had wanted to do it all herself. Perhaps it was because she had wanted to spend as much time with her daughter as she could, knowing, or sensing, that their time together was going to be short. Either way it had been Lila who had sat with Gabby at the piano, who had got her into the bath, who had led her through her prayers and read the story. And when her health declined and Lila became unable to do these things, Oscar took over.

Tonight, after they had recited an Our Father and a Hail Mary, Gabby remained kneeling. Normally she darted up and into bed, excited to commence story time. Oscar gave her a curious look, and the child said, "Daddy?"

"Yeah?"

"Can Grammy live with us?"

The question wasn't entirely unexpected. First there had been the two "dancing show" nights. More recently, Stella had begun to play card and board games with the child after school—Parcheesi, checkers, Uno, Go Fish. And today grandmother and granddaughter had baked muffins. Without a doubt Gabby was loving her Grammy. And that, Oscar now had to admit, maybe wasn't so bad. Yes, on this issue he was coming around. For the fact was, apart from himself, Duncan, and Bonnie, Stella was the only other family that Gabby had in the area. All of Lila's family were on the West Coast. And while as a kid Oscar's own experience of family life hadn't been that great, he was nonetheless convinced of its potential. Its potential for connection and community. Its potential for security and love. That said, Stella was Stella. In addition to her bad behavior and her questionable influence, it now appeared she might be using the child to get something Oscar wasn't quite prepared to give. Either way, his main concern was that Gabby not get hurt.

He said, "She does live with us."

"No, I mean forever."

"Forever?"

"Yes."

"Well, the thing is, bunny, Grammy is probably going to be moving soon. Any day now."

"Why?"

"Because she needs her own place. It's small here, right? There's only one bathroom."

"So?"

"*So* … you know. It's inconvenient. For everybody."

"Can't you make another one?"

"Another bathroom?"

The child nodded.

"Well … it's not that easy."

"Why?"

"For one thing, it's expensive … But that's not the point. The point is that Grammy is basically just visiting us. For her, it's like a vacation. And at some point vacations end and you have to go home."

"But she doesn't have a home. That's what you said."

"I did?"

"Mm-hm. You said she used to live in Hanover but now she doesn't. If she's looking for a new home, why can't it be here?"

ELEVEN

On Thursday afternoon Oscar got a text from Walter: "Can you pick me up at the store on your way to the Y?"

Oscar wrote back: "Sure. What's up?"

"You'll see when you get here."

And when Oscar pulled into the parking lot in front of Big Walter's Provisions, he saw that something indeed was up. Walter came out of the store just as Oscar was getting out of the Sorolla.

"What happened?" Oscar said.

One of the store's large plate-glass windows was covered by a sheet of plywood, and on the plywood was spray-painted, in black capital letters,

WALTER BANG

SEXUAL PREDATOR

"I don't know," Walter said. "I'm still trying to figure it out."

"Not Pam?" Oscar said doubtfully, thinking of the waitress from the Brewhouse, the one who had accused Walter of commenting on her "melons."

"No, no," Walter said mildly. "I thought about that but … she's not the type. Too laid-back. This was a real psycho. Has to be a guy. First he—or someone else—threw a brick through the window early Monday morning, around two a.m. The alarm went off and the cops came, and then they called me. I had the insurance guy over that day and then I had someone in about the window, but he said he couldn't get a replacement till Friday, so they boarded it up. Well, I show up this morning and I see this," he said, gesturing to the graffiti.

From the street behind them came two emphatic honks of a car horn. Oscar and Walter turned around. A guy in a 4x4 pickup truck, with both his arm and his ebullient face sticking out of the driver-side window, was passing by at a reduced speed. In a deep New Hampshire accent he cried out, "Go get 'em Wall-*taaah!*" The man laughed and waved.

Walter returned the wave but not the laugh, calling back, "Beano!"

The man—"Beano," evidently—gave his horn another two honks and sped off. A good-sized American flag, mounted on the bed of the truck, flapped vigorously as he went.

Without comment Walter turned back to Oscar, resuming their conversation: "No, I don't know who did it. But when I find the little bastard, he's gonna wish his father had pulled out, that's for damn sure ... And it's not just this. He got my car too."

"Your car?"

"Yeah. That's why I texted you. I'm on foot at the moment. This all happened last night. At about three a.m. I woke up in a daze—still half cocked, to tell you the truth. I thought I heard glass smashing and a car alarm but I wasn't sure if it was a dream or what. Then by the time I realized it was real, it was too late. I ran to the window and saw my car was lit up, lights flashing and the alarm still going, but no one was there. I go outside and I see the thing's all smashed up—front window, side window, back window, some of the lights. The car's still in the driveway. The claims guy is coming tomorrow."

"You have no idea who it was?"

"No."

"And why 'sexual predator'?"

"No clue. The cops asked me the same thing."

"Did you tell them about Pam?"

"No. I'm telling you, it's not her. You got to remember, I deal with the public every day. It could be anyone." Walter's eye shifted away from Oscar and he said, "Hi Mrs. Spinelli."

An elderly woman came up to them, and for some reason she addressed Oscar rather than Walter. Oscar had never seen her before.

"I've been coming to this store since nineteen seventy-six," she said, staring up at him with grave concern, "before Walter's father even bought the place. A Greek family owned it then. The Kefalases. Nice people. Though the daughter gave them trouble. But I've *never* seen anything like this." She looked at the spray-painted message, then looked back at Oscar, intently awaiting his response.

"Yes," he said. "It is something."

The woman nodded, satisfied, then focused again on the graffiti. " 'Sexual predator,' " she said, reading the words aloud in a slow, reflective voice. "Now why do you think they would write that?" She turned to Walter.

As if caught off guard, Walter shrugged and nervously glanced away. "I have no idea," he said. "It's crazy, obviously. Slander."

Watching Walter closely, the old woman's eyes narrowed and she said, "Hmmmm."

* * *

After they played hoops, Oscar and Walter walked over to Froggie's Tap Room, their new watering hole. Heidi the waitress took their order and brought two beers. Walter knocked back his first gulp, then asked Oscar how things were going with Stella. Oscar gave him the update: the tour of Riverside Pines, the muffin-baking incident, the afternoon board-game sessions, and also how Stella had begun giving Gabby a hug before bed.

Grinning, Walter said, "Sounds like someone realized living with you is a better deal than living in a piss pot."

Oscar just smiled.

"You think it's all an act?" Walter said.

"I think she recognized a potential ally, and now she's working hard to secure the bond. Which she's doing quite well, by the way. Gabby's asked me a few times now if 'Grammy' can live with us."

Heidi came with the burgers and set down the plates. To Walter she said, "We're out of mayonnaise today." Walter always ordered his burger the same way: medium rare with lettuce, tomato, onion, and extra mayonnaise. "Is that OK?" she said.

Visibly irritated, Walter said, "No. It isn't."

Heidi shrugged as if to say, "Oh well," and walked off.

"Unbelievable," Walter grumbled. He picked up his burger, took a bite, and frowned. To Oscar he said, "So what about another retirement home? For your mother."

Munching on a fry, Oscar said, "I've called every one in the area. Most of them she can't afford, and the ones she can are currently filled up. We're on a few waiting lists."

"Duncan still won't help?"

"No."

"What about your step-brother and -sister?"

"They're not interested. They don't even want to talk to her."

"Popular woman."

Oscar bit into his burger.

"So what are you going to do?" Walter said.

"I'm not sure. At first I wanted her gone ... But she's been behaving. No smoking or vaping in front of Gabby, no shenanigans with Harold in the house. And she's been treating Gabby well, and Gabby's happy. And also, school's ending soon. Next week. That means Gabby's home all day and I get much less work done, watching her and everything else."

"So you're thinking this might work for you too."

"Possibly. I've been thinking about a couple options. One is that she could stay through the summer, or maybe longer, and in return she could help out with Gabby. If she could watch her for half the day, I'd be very happy. I'm just a little wary, you know?"

"I don't blame you. Your mom's not exactly what you might call 'babysitter material.' And I mean no offense."

"None taken."

"And what's the other option?"

"The other option involves Harold Buckett ..."

TWELVE

"Grammy, Harold—watch!"

Drinks in hand, Stella and Harold watched. Oscar too.

Mindy the dog, in a frenzy of anticipation, was barking mani-acally. Gabby, holding a red kickball, turned to face the dog from about six feet away. In an underhand motion the child tossed the ball up into the air toward the dog. Springing up off the ground, Mindy met the ball with the crown of her head and sent it arcing back through the air and into Gabby's hands.

With a proud smile, the child looked at her audience.

"Impressive," Stella said.

"Do it again," Harold said with enthusiasm.

Gabby did it several more times, with the dog barking wildly between each toss.

It was Sunday afternoon and the four of them, plus Mindy, were out in the backyard. Stella and Harold sat in plastic chairs while Oscar stood at the grill, cooking T-bone steaks, au gratin potatoes in tin-foil wraps, and a single veggie burger. The idea for this little get together had been Oscar's. Inspired by Stella's crafty maneuvers with Gabby, he had begun to see his own potential ally in Harold Buckett. More specifically, he had begun to wonder if lovestruck Harold might not make an honest woman of Stella—

and provide her with a new home. It would be, Oscar felt, the perfect dénouement: the happy couple at the altar, and this little family drama resolved. Given the romantic angle, surely even Gabby would approve.

* * *

Now seated at the picnic table, the four of them were eating off paper plates. Harold in particular seemed happy with his meal. In effusive tones he was complimenting Oscar on his grilling skills: "This steak is excellent. You got it just right. Juicy, tender —it's perfect. Incredible flavor. *Mmm* ... Fantastic!"

"I'm glad you like it," Oscar said, half fearing that Harold's eyes might roll back in his head.

"And how's your veggie burger?" Harold asked Gabby.

Gabby said it was good. "Do you want a bite?"

"*Oh* ... no, no," Harold said as if caught by surprise. "Thank you. I'm all set. It looks good though."

Gabby smiled, and with amused curiosity she continued to watch Harold Buckett. She had never known anyone like him before.

Shifting to a new topic, Harold said to the child, "So I hear you play the piano. Your Grammy says you're pretty good."

"*Very* good," Stella corrected him. "She's the best piano player I ever heard."

Looking very pleased at this, and with herself, Gabby said, "I can play Beethoven *and* Mozart."

"Gabby, don't brag," Oscar said.

"Do you know any Kenny Rogers?" Harold said.

"*Who?*"

"Kenny Rogers. The Gambler. Now *there's* a singer."

"Does he play the piano?"

"No. He has a band," Stella said. "He did some songs with Dolly Parton."

"I'd like to do some songs with Dolly Parton," Harold said with a rascally look and a low, rumbly laugh.

"I'm sure you would," Stella said wryly, giving him the eye.

Clueless as to the cause of this merriment, but not wanting to be left out, Gabby said, "Who's Dolly Parton?"

"She's a singer," Oscar said, not exactly thrilled with the direction of this conversation. "I'll show you some of her videos on YouTube ... So Harold, what line of work were you in?"

"I worked for the city, mostly."

"Beauville?"

"Yep. Started out in the parks with one of the crews, then I went over to Public Works for twenty-five years."

"Well," Oscar said, sounding impressed. "You must have a nice pension, then."

"I get by."

"You ever marry?"

Stella stopped chewing and gave Oscar a sharp look.

"I guess your mother never told you," Harold said.

"Told me what?"

"*Harold*," Stella said.

"I've been in love with her since high school. We were sweethearts at Beauville High. Class of '64, the both of us."

Oscar knew nothing about this.

"Then in '65 I was drafted," Harold continued. *"Vietnam.* It changed everything. I wasn't there for more than a month when I was wounded."

"He got hit by a palm tree," Stella said with a smirk.

"A palm tree?" Oscar said.

"Friendly fire mortar shell," Harold said. "The damn tree fell right on me. Broke my hip and two ribs, punctured a lung, and cut me all up. The bark on those things is rough as hell—*oh,* sorry," he added with a glance at Gabby, as if to apologize for his language. "Anyway, luckily it hit me from behind."

"That's because he was lying on the ground, face first," Stella said.

"Just like everybody else," Harold said. "Someone yelled 'incoming!' and we all took cover. Two men died in that blast. I was laid up for months. And then one day I got a letter from Mom saying Stella had married Buddy Boyle—one of my old pals."

"I never promised you anything," Stella said.

"I know," Harold admitted. "But that doesn't mean it didn't hurt."

Stella looked away with haughty disdain, but also a hint of pleasure.

"So I'm devastated by this," Harold said, continuing the story as though he'd told it many times before, "but life goes on, and eventually I get married. But as soon as I do, I hear that Stella and Buddy have split, and I realize that I still love Stella—that it's her I want to be with, not my new wife."

"Oh, no," Oscar said.

"Yep."

"Maybe we should talk about something else," Oscar added, discreetly nodding in Gabby's direction.

But the child piped up: "Are you still married?"

"No. Ellie passed eight years ago now, God bless her. We had a good life. Three kids, five grandchildren."

"Are you going to marry Grammy?"

"Ha!" Stella said.

"*Gabby*," Oscar said, though he quickly turned to Harold, alert and hopeful.

"Maybe," Harold said, looking distressed.

"Maybe?" Oscar said.

"Harold's a mama's boy," Stella said.

"Stell and Mom don't really get along," Harold said.

"We can't stand each other," Stella said.

"It goes back to Buddy Boyle," Harold said.

"But why does it matter?" Oscar said, the hope fading from his face.

"Because they live together," Stella said.

Oscar—and Gabby—looked at Harold.

"Mom moved in with Ellie and me when she turned eighty. She's ninety-four now."

"She'll outlive us all," Stella grumbled. "And he refuses to put her in a home."

Again they all looked at Harold.

Almost apologetically he said, "She gave me life. How could I put her in a home?"

All at once Oscar felt very self-conscious. He lowered his eyes, not wanting to see his mother. And when he looked up, he saw that his daughter was looking at *him*.

* * *

Late the next morning, Oscar found Stella out on the back deck. Seated in one of the yard chairs, oxygen tank at her side, she exhaled a plume of strawberry-scented vapor as he opened the screen door. She looked up at him but said nothing. Oscar sat in one the chairs, facing the yard.

"Wow, what a day," he said in a chipper, sociable tone. "I love this weather." It was sunny and warm, around seventy degrees.

Stella just said, "Yep."

Smiling agreeably, Oscar continued with the sociable tone: "You seem to like it out here." Since her arrival Stella had been spending a lot of time on the deck, and not just for vaping. Shaded from the sun by two towering oaks she liked to read her supermarket romance novels and talk to Harold on the phone. And sometimes she just sat, taking in the view.

"It's nice," she said.

"Better than Riverside Pines?"

She gave him a leery glance.

"Anyway, Ma, there's something I want to talk to you about."

"*Here we go*," she said dramatically. "I knew it!" She brought the e-cig to her lips and let out another white plume.

"It's nothing bad, Ma. What I'm wondering is—do you like living here?"

She looked at him, guarded and questioning. "It's all right."

"Good. And what about Gabby? What do you think about her?"

"What is this?" Stella snapped, her eyes now hostile and filled with mistrust.

"It's nothing, Ma. We're just talking. I'm just curious to know what your thoughts are about Gabby."

Slowly, the tension eased from Stella's face. "I was never one for children," she said. "Didn't see the point of them. But that was the thing—'have kids!' In those days, even men wanted them. But *they* didn't have to take care of them."

Oscar nodded. "I appreciate hearing that, Ma. Thank you. But what about Gabby?"

"Gabby," Stella said with a ruminative air. "She's … she's grown on me."

"She's grown on you," Oscar repeated, watching her.

Stella averted her eyes and made a slight shrug. "Yeah," she said, almost as though she was embarrassed to admit it.

Oscar observed his mother closely, keeping in mind her long history of theatrics and wily connivance. In this instance, however, her words and demeanor seemed genuine. So he said, "I'm glad to hear it, because I know she really likes you. You seem to make her happy … Anyway, as you know, school's ending this week, and what I'm wondering is, if you might be interested in helping out with her this summer."

" 'Helping out'?" Stella said suspiciously.

"Yes. I'm thinking you could keep living here, and in return you could watch Gabby in the mornings while I work. In the afternoons she'll be going to the park, so you'll be free. I'm also thinking you could make us lunch."

"*Lunch?*"

"Yes."

"This sounds like a job to me. I'm retired!"

Oscar fired back: "Ma, remember when Duncan and I were kids? What was your favorite line? When you made us do the dishes and clean the house, and when we got older and we had to cook and do the laundry—what did you always say when we asked why we had to do it? What did you always say? *'This isn't a hotel.'* Remember? Well, right back at you: this isn't a hotel, Ma. You've been living here for almost a month now and you've yet to offer to help with anything. I'm happy to have you, and you're welcome to stay … for the time being. We'll see how it goes. But for now it would be nice if you could help out."

"What would I have to cook?"

"Nothing fancy. Sandwiches, soups, chips. If you can bake muffins, you can certainly heat up a can of soup."

She reflected on this. "And what time?"

"When I'm working at home, I like to break around twelve-thirty."

"I'll miss *Restless Hearts*," she said, referring to one of her favorite soaps.

"We can record it. You won't miss a thing."

Stella gazed out into the backyard. A blue jay was calling from one of the trees. In the distance a lawnmower droned.

"All right," she said.

"Good," Oscar said. "But I need to know one thing. Can I depend on you?"

She looked at him, paused, then said, "Yes."

* * *

A week passed, and then another, and remarkably, Oscar had no complaints. Things were going well. Better than expected. In the mornings Stella watched Gabby while the child read or practiced piano or played in the backyard with neighborhood kids. At twelve-thirty, on those days when Oscar was working in the studio, he emerged to find lunch waiting on the kitchen table. Together, all three Perillouxs sat down for their midday meal. Against the odds, Stella was keeping to her word. On several afternoons she had even offered to accompany Gabby to the park.

A two minute walk from the house, Bennet Park had a duck pond, a huge pool, clean changing rooms, baseball fields, and basketball and tennis courts. Gabby went there for swimming lessons and other supervised activities: art class, kickball, the occasional field trip. On one of the afternoons that Stella had walked over with the child, Oscar had waited an hour and then set out after them. He wanted to make sure everything was copacetic. No mischief, no funny business. And there, unobserved from a thicket of trees fifty yards away, he spied Stella and Harold. They sat on a bench facing the pool, watching as Gabby and a bunch of other kids played and splashed in the water. To Oscar, this was a welcome sight. He liked Harold and felt he must be a good influence on Stella. Or at least, the best possible influence she was likely to get, all things considered. Either way Harold seemed a decent, responsible guy, and his presence in the park meant there was yet another adult on hand to keep an eye out for Gabby.

So pleased was Oscar by all of these developments that he decided to throw a Fourth of July barbecue. He, Stella, Gabby, and

Harold would grill out in the backyard and then, at dusk, head over to Memorial Stadium for the city's annual fireworks. Harold had even offered to bring beer. But on the evening of July first, Oscar got an unexpected call.

Skipping the small talk, Duncan got right to it: "I'm having a big cookout at my place on the Fourth. Fireworks, caterers, open bar. I'd like you to come."

If the call was unexpected, this invitation was doubly so. Apart from the occasional Thanksgiving or Christmas dinner, and Bonnie's annual birthday extravaganzas—last year's iteration had included a magician with a half-naked female assistant, a sword-swallower, a fire-eater, and three clowns—Oscar had been invited to Duncan's home maybe two or three times since he'd moved back to Beauville. With this in mind he said, "Why?"

"*Why?* What do you mean, 'why'? It's a holiday ... I'd like to see you."

Duncan may have achieved a great worldly success, outfoxing his competition and coaxing countless Granite Staters to buy his cars and trucks, but when it came to telling white lies he was about as convincing as Gabby.

"I'm very touched," Oscar said. "But I already have plans."

"Cancel them."

"I can't. I'm having a barbecue."

"With who?"

"Ma, Harold, and Gabby. It's all set."

"*Ma's* still at your place?" Duncan said, incredulous.

"Yes. She's going to be staying through the summer."

There was a long silence, and Oscar knew Duncan likely was fuming. He said, "Hello?"

Calmly, even politely, Duncan said, "Could you come just for an hour or two?"

Obviously, something was up. The politeness was a dead give-away. "Mmmm … I don't think so."

"Dammit Oscar, it's just for an hour!"

Oscar sighed. "What time does it start?"

"Six."

"Sorry. That's when mine starts. Ask me next year."

"This can't wait till next year!"

"Duncan, what's going on?" Oscar said, in a let's-cut-the-bull-shit tone.

"It's Margot."

"Margot?"

"Yes. She's coming to the cookout."

"OK," Oscar said, now puzzled.

"For weeks I've been trying to repair things with her, and now I think she's coming around."

Oscar highly doubted that, yet still he was puzzled. "I'm happy to hear it Duncan, but what does this have to do with me?"

"When I invited her she asked if you were coming, and I said, 'Of course not.' I figured you were the last person she wanted to see. But she said, 'Oh, that's too bad.' I said, 'You *want* him to come?' And she said, 'Yes, I'd like to see him.' I said, '*Why?*' And she said she wants to talk to you about the birthday party. She said she felt bad about it, the way it ended, though I don't know why. As far as I'm concerned, she had every right to yell at you Oscar. *Every right*. But that's the kind of person she is. She's got a big heart. So I said, 'He'll come. I'll make sure of it.' And then she said she'd come. So there it is. Now will you do this for me?"

"Well … I suppose I could ask Ma and Harold if they want to go—"

"*Ma and Harold?* No way. No. Oscar, that's impossible. This isn't a family thing. It's a business thing. I'm rebranding the company, and I'm going to have my entire management team there with their families. So no—Ma and Harold *Buckett* are not invited."

"Then I'm sorry. I can't go. Tell Margot she can call anytime. She has my number."

"Oscar, come on!"

"Bye Duncan." He hung up.

Ten minutes later, Duncan rang back—just as Oscar knew he would. Duncan said Stella and Harold could come to the cookout, but only if Oscar promised to keep them sober and away from the other guests.

Oscar said he would do his best.

THIRTEEN

Duncan's estate sat high atop a hill in the rural outskirts of Beauville. At the entrance was a large wrought-iron gate, which opened and closed via remote control. Oscar had always found the thing pretentious, and frankly ridiculous. Who did Duncan think he was, Bruce Wayne? Michael Jackson? Presently the gate was open, permitting entry to the long asphalt drive that wound up through woods to the house. On either side of the drive were dozens of parked cars. Oscar found a spot for the Sorolla, then he and Gabby continued on foot.

"Who are all these cars?" Gabby asked.

"Uncle Duncan's employees."

As they went around a bend of trees, the house came into view. Duncan had had it custom-built five years earlier. He'd bought the hundred-plus acres of land and the old farm that came with it, and promptly demolished the place and got to work on his dream home. The result, alas, was something of an eyesore, an enormous nouveau-riche castle that looked like a cross between a log cabin and a modernist ski chalet—Abe Lincoln meets Le Corbusier. There were thick machine-cut logs, walls of gray concrete, and huge panes of glass.

Standing outside the front door was a college-age kid in black pants, white shirt, and black bowtie. On his chest was a large round pin, about the size of a grapefruit, that read:

Perilloux Motors

Making a Better World

"Welcome to the Perilloux residence," the kid said with a friendly smile.

"Thanks," Oscar said, as he passed by and continued toward the house.

"*Excuse me*—sir?"

Oscar and Gabby stopped and looked back.

The kid reached into a plastic bag he was holding and pulled out two pins, just like the one he was wearing. "Here you go," he said, holding the pins out to Oscar and making the same friendly smile.

"We're all set," Oscar said, rejecting the gift and turning to go.

"Mr. Perilloux wants everyone to wear a pin," the kid said, now with some authority, and a bit of a smirk.

"Is that so?" Oscar said. He looked at Gabby. "Come on, let's go."

But Gabby wasn't ready to go. "Daddy, can I get a pin?"

"No. You're a person. Not a billboard."

They went into the house. A handful of guests, all wearing Perilloux Motors pins, stood in the cavernous foyer, holding drinks, chatting, and inspecting the home's rustic décor. To the left a wide maple stairway went up to the second floor, and to the right you could see into the main living room, a lofty open-plan space with several sofas, armchairs, a huge fieldstone fireplace, and a giant chandelier made of dozens of deer antlers. There were oriental rugs, gold-framed landscape paintings—two by Oscar, thank you very much—and, hard to miss, a stuffed buffalo standing on four legs. At the opposite end of the foyer was another doorway and a large wall of glass that looked onto the backyard, now filled with guests.

As Oscar and Gabby crossed the room and stepped out into the dense noisy crowd, the child reached for his hand. Seeing her nervous face, Oscar gave her a reassuring smile. "You OK?"

She nodded.

"We'll find Bonnie," he added.

But as Oscar scanned the throng—adults and children, standing around the pool, loading up at the food tables and the bar, and mingling in the spaces in between—his roving eye searched not for his niece but for *her*. Margot.

Then from behind he heard: "Hello Gabby."

Oscar turned, and felt a rush of happiness.

"Hi Mrs. Saadeh!" Gabby said.

"How are you?"

"Gooood. Are Zora and Sana here?"

"No, they're with their aunt and cousins today."

"Oh."

Margot turned to Oscar and they said hello. Both were smiling, and for some moments they just looked at each other.

"Daddy, I see Bonnie."

"OK. I'll be here."

The child ran off.

Still looking at Margot, Oscar noticed the pin. She was wearing one too. Not a good sign. He said, "How was France?"

"It was great. One of my cousins got married. He lives in Lyon, and we stayed for a couple weeks, visiting family. Then I took the girls to Paris and other places. Versailles, Chartres, Disneyland—" She chortled, as though amused by the absurdity. "It was fun."

They talked more about the trip and then Oscar asked if she was still going to Sacred Heart. He hadn't seen her there for more than a month, since before Gabby's birthday party.

"No, my sister has a place on Winnipesaukee, and we've been staying up there since we got back. We go to a church in Laconia."

"I see. Well that's good."

"Yeah, the kids like it up there, and they're close with their cousins. But how have you been?"

"I've been—"

"*Little brother*," said a familiar voice, teeming with swagger. Giving Oscar a look of airy condescension, Duncan came up and planted himself close beside Margot, as if to mark his territory. Beaming extravagantly, standing erect and proud, his whole being exuded an air of superiority—and triumph.

Oscar understood. This was a great moment for Duncan. Here he was, king of this palace, surrounded by his attendant princes—or more likely, his serfs—all come to pay court. And he may even have won back his queen. In light of such a regal victory, "little brother" Oscar had been exposed as a mere knave. Duncan's gloating expression seemed to say, "Sibling rivalry? More like sibling rout!"

Oscar, however, was in no mood for it. Certainly not in front of Margot. Very coolly he said, "Well—it's the King of Perilloux Motors ... How are you Duncan?"

"I'm good," he said, looking tremendously pleased. Pleased with himself. Pleased with life. Pleased with everything.

"Great party," Oscar said, taking in the scene.

"Thank you."

"And I love the pins," Oscar added, glancing at the Perilloux Motors / Making a Better World pin on Duncan's own chest.

Duncan registered the sarcasm, but refused to be provoked. Maintaining his composure he said, "I'm rebranding the company. It's our new motto."

Mulling this, Oscar nodded. "And how exactly are you going to 'make a better world'? By selling more cars?"

Margot laughed, but quickly stifled it.

Duncan glared at his brother, his stolid facade beginning to crack. "We're going to take a more active role in the community. With Margot's input, I've come up with some ideas on how we can help the homeless."

"The *homeless*?" Oscar said, thinking of their mother.

"Yes," Duncan said, becoming uneasy, as if sensing Oscar's thoughts. "My team and I are going to be exploring other issues as well. The environment ... diversity ... And so on. It's about becoming more socially aware. A company that cares."

Oscar was astounded. This was not the brother he remembered. "So what," he said, "you've become 'woke'?" To Margot he added, "In college he was president of the Ayn Rand Society."

With a lofty smirk Duncan said, "Oscar, stick to painting, OK?" To Margot he added, "He knows nothing about making money. Or politics. Obviously."

"You're the expert," Oscar said. "*Obviously.*"

Caught up amid this fraternal sniping, Margot appeared ill at ease. To Oscar she said, "Are you ... *apolitical?*"

"No. Not at all. I'm just wary of people who seek power. You know, criminals and sociopaths."

Again, and despite herself, Margot laughed. Duncan did not.

"I'm exaggerating," Oscar said. "But you get the idea."

"Oscar's an *Independent*," Duncan sneered. "Thinks he's too good for either party. Too high-minded."

"Yeah, God forbid someone should want to think for themself," Oscar said. "Always a bad sign."

"It's because you're a loner. You always have been."

"I'm not a loner. I'm just not a joiner. There's a difference."

Margot, now with a playful air, said, "You're a Marxist."

As if by some mental osmosis, some deep psychic connection, Oscar got it. Making an exaggerated comic grin, he raised an imaginary cigar to the side of his face and waggled his eyebrows, saying, "Egg-*xactly!*"

There was more laughter from Margot, her eyes filling with glee.

It was too much for Duncan. In heated tones he said, "He's no Marxist! He's more Catholic than the pope!"

"She meant Groucho," Oscar said calmly. "Not Karl."

"*What?*"

"Groucho Marx. He said he would never join a club that would have him."

Duncan's face went blank with incomprehension, and for some moments he stared in silence at Oscar, his eyes befuddled. Then he said, "I don't get you. I really don't."

A young guy in a polo shirt and khakis, mid-twenties, came up to Duncan. With a mix of servility and self-importance he apologized for interrupting. Then, noticing Oscar, he said, "Did you not get a pin?"

"I'm all set," Oscar said.

"I'll get you one," the guy insisted, glancing nervously at Duncan.

"It's OK," Duncan said irritably. "What do you want?"

The guy leaned close to Duncan and whispered something. Duncan frowned, muttered some order, and the guy darted off toward the house.

"Who was that?" Oscar said.

"One of my assistants."

"*One* of them?"

Duncan ignored this and said, "Ma's here, Oscar. You need to take care of it."

"*Excuse me?*" Oscar said, put off by the high-handed tone.

"Your mother?" Margot said innocently. "Oh, I'd love to meet her."

"No!" Duncan blurted, horrified. "I mean ... aren't you hungry? It's getting late. Let's get something to eat. We can say hello later."

And suddenly, there was a commotion: a single raised voice, and many people turning to stare. Oscar, Margot, and Duncan did too. Emerging from the house, and wheeling her oxygen tank behind her, Stella was berating Duncan's assistant.

"Get away from me you clown! You dog-faced flunky!"

"Ma'am ... *Ma'am*," the guy said in a hushed, flustered voice.

"Beat it kid! Scram!"

And coming behind them, with a Perilloux Motors pin affixed to his chest, was Harold Buckett. Corpulent as ever, and wearing one of his too-small T-shirts, he appeared extremely uncomfortable, his expression sheepish and stiff.

Duncan had turned very pale. In a near-begging tone he said, "Oscar, *please*."

* * *

As he made his way through the crowd, Oscar noted all the many different stares aimed at his mother and Harold. Stares of astonishment. Stares of ridicule. Stares of hilarity. Stares of contempt. Without question, the newcomers had gotten everyone's attention.

To Duncan's assistant, still hovering at Stella's side, Oscar said, "Thanks—I've got this."

The guy glowered at Oscar, his eyes filling with resentment. First he'd been publicly abused by Stella, and now his authority was being overridden by this pin-less guest. With a show of injured dignity, he averted his gaze and stormed off.

"Who was that jerk?" Stella growled. "He wanted me and Harold to stay in the kitchen. He said he would bring us all the food and drink we wanted. You know what I told him, don't you? The little prick."

For his part, Harold looked deeply chagrined—cowed and shamed, as though he'd not expected this grand setting or this hostile reception.

"Nice to see you Harold," Oscar said, making full eye contact and hoping to put him at ease.

"It's an impressive home," Harold said, taking in the surroundings and reverting to the formal tone Oscar remembered from the first time they'd met. "Exquisite taste."

"Yes," Oscar agreed. "Very." Then, turning to his mother he said, "So you decided to come."

That morning, after originally having agreed to attend the cookout, Stella had abruptly changed her mind. "Duncan can go to hell," she'd said. Now she said, "Sligo's was dead. So we thought we'd check this out … Though this looks dead too, with all these stiffs."

Oscar looked around. Most of the guests were no longer staring. They had returned to their drinks and their conversations.

"Where's Duncan?" Stella said. "Is he hiding?"

"He's busy, Ma. He'll say hello when he can."

"I'm sure he will."

Gabby came running and said hello to both Stella and Harold. Harold seemed especially pleased to see her—another friendly face in an otherwise unfriendly crowd. Then Bonnie approached, and Oscar instantly got a bad feeling.

With a cold predatory look, the child homed in on Harold. "Who are you?" she said.

"I'm Harold," he said, in a kind voice and with a kind smile.

"You're *fat!*"

"*Bonnie!*" Oscar said. "What a horrible thing to say. Apologize, right now!"

"*No!* This is *my* house. I can say whatever I want!" She gave Oscar a nasty look then turned and marched off.

This new outburst drew more attention. All around them people were gawking, and laughing, with few of them even bothering to conceal their mirth.

Oscar was mortified. "Harold, I'm sorry."

"That little bitch!" Stella said.

"*Ma,*" Oscar said, thinking of Gabby.

As for Harold, it was yet another blow. He was shaken, his eyes stunned, his cheeks flaming from humiliation.

Again Oscar apologized.

"Oh, it's nothing," Harold said, forcing a brave smile. "She was probably just kidding."

"No she wasn't," Stella said.

"Why don't we get some food," Oscar said. "We'll get a table and sit down."

* * *

Out beyond the pool were thirty or so cloth-covered tables arranged on the green lawn. From the buffet area people got their food—lobsters, steamers, steaks, corn on the cob—and sat where they pleased. At their table, Stella and Harold were already on their second round of drinks. The booze had lightened their moods, as had the food. Wearing plastic bibs, they were each working away at a boiled-red crustacean on their plate, cracking claws and tails and eating the butter-drenched meat with great relish.

"This is a fine lobster," Harold grandly announced. "A two-pounder at least. Maybe two and a half. But still very tender."

Duncan had yet to stop by to say hello, and in fact Oscar hadn't even seen his brother since the arrival of their mother. Margot, on the other hand, was very much present. From his seat at the table Oscar had watched how she, now solo, had mingled and circulated on her own, talking with different people, laughing and smiling and clearly enjoying herself. Presently, she found her way over to the Perilloux table.

Oscar shot to his feet and made the introductions. Harold, whether following Oscar's lead or adhering to his own chival-rous code, likewise stood. He offered his hand and even made a slight bow, saying, "The pleasure is all mine." As the two of them shook, a cheery but somewhat perplexed look came over Margot's face, as if she wasn't quite sure if Harold was joking.

"And who are you with?" Stella said distrustfully, eyeing Margot and her Perilloux Motors pin.

"I came by myself," she said pleasantly.

"You work for Duncan?"

"No."

"They're friends," Oscar said.

"And I know Oscar through church," she added, glancing at him.

He couldn't help but smile.

Still with the courtly tone, Harold said, "Would you care to join us?"

"Thank you. I would," Margot said, playfully adding a touch of courtliness to her own voice.

Theirs was a round table, with six chairs. To Oscar's left sat Gabby, then Stella, then Harold. Between Oscar and Harold were two empty chairs. Assessing the situation, Margot opted for the chair next to Harold. Oscar wondered why, but soon felt he understood.

"So are you two married?" Margot said, promptly engaging the elder couple.

Harold's face lit up with pleasure. Stella's face darkened.

"Hell no," she said.

Still beaming, Harold said, "Maybe someday."

"Ours is a Plutonic relationship," Stella said. "Mostly."

Margot's eyes widened and she bit her lower lip, as though forcing herself not to grin.

"Ma," Oscar said gently. "It's *Platonic*. Yours is a 'Platonic relationship' … 'Mostly.' "

"What's that?" Gabby said.

"It means … they're special friends," Oscar said.

The answer delighted the child, and she turned her smiling face to her Grammy.

Harold then related the tragic tale of his nearly sixty years of love for Stella Perilloux, including his experience in Vietnam. Stella interjected the part about Harold being "hit by a palm tree." This led to her going on about her father, Corporal McTavish. "*He* was hit by a bullet, not a tree."

"Oh—I'm so sorry," Margot said.

"He died a hero," Stella said, "fighting for his country. But he gave better than he got. Six reds he killed—*with his bare hands*. Six! I'd like to see Duncan do that!"

"Ma."

"What? That's your history. You think all these stuck-ups would be here mooching off Duncan if it wasn't for people like your grandfather? They'd all be in concentration camps, that's where they'd be."

"OK, Ma," Oscar said. "Thank you."

With a righteous air, Stella took a pull off her gin.

Margot's eyes shone with a merry sparkle. Evidently she was enjoying the conversation—or at least finding it entertaining. Turning to Stella she said, "Do you live in Beauville, Mrs. Perilloux?"

"I do. I was born here, and I live here now. With this one," she added, nodding at Oscar.

Oscar tried not to wince. He had been hoping to keep this information secret, at least for the time being. But so much for that.

For her part, Margot made no comment. Instead she gave Oscar a long, enigmatic look. A thoughtful, speculative look— her mind working, deliberating. Was she, once again, writing him off as a loser? Concocting a polite exit line? Wondering why, in the first place, she had even agreed to come to this cookout? Oscar couldn't tell. At last she looked away, turning to Harold.

"And where do you live?" she said to him.

Flushed from drink and good cheer, Harold seemed immensely gratified by the question. With a mix of gravity and gusto he proceeded to narrate, in great detail, the rest of his life story not covered by his love for Stella Perilloux and his stint in Vietnam.

* * *

Dusk had begun to fall. Fifty yards away, in the rolling pasture that stretched for several acres behind the house, were two parked vans. It was the fireworks crew, four guys who were just about finished setting up their equipment. Over a portable PA, Duncan's assistant announced that Duncan was going to say a few words. "Please gather by the pool."

"This should be good," Stella grumbled.

Harold helped her up, and Gabby, excited for the fireworks, went on ahead of them. As everyone drifted away from the tables, Margot asked Oscar to hold back.

Once they were alone she said, "It was nice meeting your mother and Harold."

"*Really?*" Oscar said, looking at her.

Margot chuckled. "Yes."

"Well, it's nice of you to say. And I appreciate how you treated them—you know, like actual human beings. I think it made their day."

"They made my day. They're very charming."

Oscar smiled, and waited.

Margot said, "So, I wanted to apologize for the birthday party. I'm sorry for what I said, and how upset I got. I guess when it comes to my girls, I can be a little … overprotective."

"I know," Oscar said. "It's one of the things I like about you."

Meeting his eye, Margot flinched. It was a subtle, just-detectable movement, but Oscar caught it, and for five, ten seconds neither of them spoke.

Oscar's heart was thumping, pounding, and he wanted to say more. He wanted to make his confession, tell Margot that he had feelings for her. But just as he finally opened his mouth to do it, the excited voice of Duncan's assistant blared over the PA: "And now, your generous host, *and employer*—the founder, president, and CEO of Perilloux Motors—*Duncan Perilloux!*"

With an anxious look, Margot said, "We should go."

* * *

They stood at the edge of the crowd. Well-fed and plenty liquored up, the assembled guests were in good spirits. Good spirits, that is, for a work function. A work function held on a national holiday. The applause that had greeted Duncan's introduction was thus neither tepid nor zealous. It struck just the right note, and Duncan appeared satisfied. Microphone in hand, he stood atop a three-foot-high dais, smiling with appreciation —and maybe a bit of *self*-appreciation.

Taking in the multitude, young and old, with their deferential faces and their Perilloux Motors pins, Duncan said, "What a day this has been … Seeing all of you and your families. Your kids. Your spouses. Your partners. Getting all the management teams together—from Parts, Financing, Servicing, and Sales—from all four dealerships in one beautiful setting … Just incredible." With an aw-shucks air he shook his head, as if overwhelmed by gratitude and humility.

"Now I know you're all excited for the fireworks," he went on. "I'm told Spider McDaniels and the guys at Beauville Fireworks have quite the show lined up for you. So I'll keep this short."

From behind a voice cried out: "Good!"

Heads turned, and there were even some muffled laughs. Standing alone at the open bar, with her air tank and a refreshed gin and tonic, was Stella Perilloux.

Oscar said "Excuse me" to Margot and went over to his mother. In a lowered voice he said, "Ma, no."

"How is it possible I gave birth to that turkey?"

"*Ma*, not now."

Stella shook her head, but went silent.

All eyes turned back to Duncan. A flicker of vexation had passed over him, but recovery came quick. He was in front of his people, his Perilloux Motors people, and in no way was he going to lose face by getting drawn into an unseemly family quarrel. From the dais, he straightened his posture and projected a winning air: composed, competent, and supremely self-assured. And for the next forty minutes he regaled his captive listeners with inspiring episodes from the history of Perilloux Motors: how at age twenty-five, as a newly minted MBA, he had arranged a novel financing scheme to purchase his first dealership; how over two decades he had grown the business from one, to two, to three, and finally to four dealerships; how his original motto for the company—"Come on by!"—had come to him in a dream; and how the company's new motto—"Making a Better World"— had come to him from a Boston advertising agency he had hired back in May.

Duncan then turned philosophical. He talked about how the internet was "constantly shrinking the planet and making us all public figures"; how consumers today were "more loyal to brands than to nationalities"; how the younger generation had "merged politics and consumption"; and how markets were "adapting to these new demands." Because of this, Duncan said, Perilloux Motors would be "increasing its philanthropic footprint to promote consciousness-raising and trending social causes."

It was at this point that something odd happened. Many in the crowd, especially those who had been fighting off boredom and fatigue, suddenly became alert. A murmur of agitated voices arose and everyone looked off to the left.

Sitting behind the wheel of a motorized toy car, and driving straight toward the crowd, was Bonnie Perilloux. The car was a bright pink convertible, about the size of a small sofa, and with its electric engine it moved quiet and slow—no more than four, five miles per hour. Yet as Bonnie approached the gathered guests, Duncan's employees and their dependents, it became clear she had no intention of stopping or altering her course. She began hitting the horn, again and again, but in a leisurely way—"beep" ... "beep" ... "beep"—as adults and children began to lurch and lunge and dart out of the way, creating a lengthening path of pandemonium. Without pause the car breezed through the throng and passed by the dais and continued on.

Thankfully, no one was struck, and because this was the boss's kid, some people tried to laugh. But others looked baffled. Still others, disturbed. For his part, Duncan was clearly disconcerted —angry, embarrassed, flustered. With strain showing on his face, he spoke into the microphone: "That's just Bonnie ... She's, uh, she's just looking for a little attention," he added, with maybe more insight than he was aware. He then glared at his assistant, and furiously motioned his head in the direction of Bonnie as she drove away. The guy promptly went after the child.

Despite this setback, Duncan soldiered on. He was on a mission, after all, and that mission was not yet complete. To the buzzing crowd he said, "So anyway—hello? ... Yes, thank you. So anyway, I'm going to wrap this up ... But before I do, I'd like to leave you with some final thoughts. Thoughts that get to the heart of why we're all here today ... What I want, is to challenge you. That's right: I want to challenge all of you, *and* myself. Everyone here. I want to challenge us all to be *better*. To be better people. To be better neighbors. To be better employees. Let us strive, each and every day, to provide our customers with the best service and the best deals and the best purchasing experience possible. Let us strive, each and every day, to pursue excellence, and to ensure that Perilloux Motors fulfills its new pledge of 'Making a Better World.' Together, we can do it. We *can* make ... a Better World. Thank you, and God bless you all." Duncan made his best billboard smile, his handsome face radiating benevolence and goodwill. Then, as if suddenly remembering something, he added, "Oh, and the bar's still open. So grab another drink and, uh, enjoy the fireworks."

The applause was scattered, and brief, and it came mostly from the front, from those nearest to Duncan's watchful eyes. Those standing in the back were already halfway to the bar.

In the general disorder Oscar gathered Gabby, Stella, and Harold. It was dark out now, and soon the first of the fireworks exploded. High overhead the colors burst in red, white, and blue, lighting up the sky. Reinvigorated by the spectacle, and also another infusion of booze, the crowd cheered and let loose many "ooohs" and "aaahs." Holding his daughter's hand, Oscar scanned the scene. But try as he might, looking all around as the fireworks continued to explode, one after the other, brilliant and loud, he could not locate Margot. She wasn't there. She was gone.

FOURTEEN

"Dad, I think birds are my new favorite animal."

"Better than monkeys?"

The child pondered this, and a look of uncertainty flickered over her face. "Maybe the same."

It was the morning after the cookout, and the three Perillouxs were seated out on the back deck. They had just finished breakfast. Oscar and Stella were sipping the last of their coffees, while Gabby held binoculars to her eyes, searching for wildlife in the backyard. As it turned out, Walter's birthday present had proved a big hit. On their regular nature walks, which Oscar and Gabby took once or twice a week, the girl was always in possession of her field glasses. Today would be no different.

"Daddy, are you ready?" she said, eager to head out.

"We'll leave after you do the dishes. And brush your teeth."

"Can I do the dishes later?"

From experience Oscar knew that "later" often meant "never." He said, "Nope."

With a slight pout the child went into the house.

"You run a tight ship," Stella said.

Oscar chuckled. "Would Corporal McTavish approve?"

Surprised by the idea of it, Stella said, "I think he would."

"You know, Ma, last night you told Margot that Grandpa Mc-Tavish killed six reds in Korea."

"I remember."

"When we were kids, it was two. The body count seems to have gone up."

"Well … I forget the exact number."

Oscar sipped from his mug. "Did you enjoy yourself yesterday?"

"It was all right. Your brother never talked to us."

"You did heckle him, Ma. During his speech."

Stella made a face, but said nothing.

"And what did you think of Margot?"

"I liked her. And if you had any brains, you'd take off that ring. A girl like that won't be single for long."

Oscar looked down at his wedding band. "Duncan likes her."

"Ha!" Stella said. "Good luck. If she's interested in him, it's for one thing only. And I don't mean sex."

Oscar smiled.

"Believe me, she's not interested in Duncan. You think she talked to Harold and me for *our* benefit?"

"Ma, come on. Yes, I do. She's a good person."

"Harold certainly thought so. He kept talking about her all the way home. I started to get jealous."

When Gabby returned, with the binoculars hanging around her neck and a small black notebook clutched in one hand, she said, "Ready!"

"You all set?" Oscar said.

"Yep!"

"Where are you going?" Stella said.

"Out near the quarries."

"How are you getting there?"

"The motorcycle!" Gabby said.

"I want to come," Stella said.

"What?" Oscar said.

"I want to go with you. I'm not staying cooped up in this house all day."

"Where would you sit?" Gabby said.

"We'll take the car," Oscar said.

"Oh, no," Stella said. "I want to go on that bike. I've been watching you guys for weeks. I want a ride too."

* * *

Oscar wheeled the motorcycle out of the garage. Gabby already had her helmet and ski goggles on. Stella wore Oscar's helmet.

"All right," he said. "Let's do this."

He helped lower Stella down into the sidecar and handed her the air tank. Then he helped Gabby get in, guiding her onto her grandmother's lap.

Stella said, "You have a bony butt, Gabby. Like two little knives."

The child grinned, abashed. "I eat a lot of food," she said.

"You need some Big Macs, is what you need."

Oscar laughed, strapped the two of them in with the seatbelt, and soon they were off. He drove careful and slow and stuck to the back roads. They passed through stretches of dense green woods and then went by a farm. Cows grazed in one of the fields, and in another the corn stalks were waist-high. With the wind in her face Stella had a serene, contented look, taking in the sights and enjoying the ride.

Because the trails he usually went to would be too difficult for her—there were hills and gullies, and rocks and roots in the paths—Oscar decided to go instead to a nature park along the river. The park was wooded and mostly unspoiled, and had a wide dirt path with a smattering of granite benches facing the water. If his mother got tired, she could stop and rest.

* * *

"Harold used to come fishing here," Stella said, after they had parked the bike and removed the helmets. "That was before they put in these trails. Now it's a pickup joint, from what I heard."

"What's that?" Gabby said.

"People come here on dates," Oscar said, giving his mother a look.

Stella went silent.

Showing not one scintilla of interest in the concept of "dating," the child moved on to more pressing matters. "Daddy, will you take my notebook?"

The previous year, Gabby had carried the notebook herself, writing down the names of the different animals as she saw them. Now, because her hands were busy with the binoculars, she required an assistant. Oscar was happy to oblige. He took possession of the notebook and pen, and, with Gabby leading the way, the three of them headed for the path.

Overhead the morning sun was already hot. Sweat formed on Oscar's skin and dampened his shirt. Yet along the path, shaded by tall pines and leafy maples and oaks, the air was fragrant and cool. It smelled of the river and damp earth; a sweet, clean smell. There was birdsong and the sound of cicadas from the trees, and from the river came the steady burbling of water flowing among exposed rocks.

They hadn't been walking for five minutes when Oscar said, "Gabby, up ahead, across the river."

The child rushed to a clearing in the trees and raised her glasses. She looked, and she looked some more. "What?"

"Keep looking."

"Oh, wow!" she said. "A heron!"

Seventy, eighty yards away, near the opposite bank of the wide river, a single great blue heron stood sunning itself in the shallows.

"Its legs are so skinny. Is he looking for fish?"

"Maybe."

"Could you write that down?"

Oscar opened the notebook and wrote:

July 5, 2019, Merrimack River

1) One great blue heron—maybe looking for fish

As soon as Oscar finished writing, Stella started hacking. It was a violent, phlegmy cough, her body convulsing again and again. Gabby turned to watch.

"Are you all right?" Oscar said.

"I'm fine. Though it's hot." Her face was flushed and she looked exhausted.

"You want to sit?" Oscar said, becoming concerned.

"Yes."

They walked back a little ways toward the parking lot, to the nearest bench.

"You go on," Stella said, after she had sat.

"No, we can wait."

"I'll be fine. It's a nice view."

Oscar hesitated.

"Go on!" she said.

"OK … we'll be back in a bit."

He and Gabby continued on. They saw a woodpecker, a couple cormorants, a thrush, a monarch butterfly, and a few chipmunks —all of which were noted down. And the two times a dog-walker approached from the opposite direction, Gabby had to pet the dog and ask the owner what its name was and other important questions.

Thinking all the while of his mother, Oscar decided to cut the walk short. "I want to check on Grammy," he said. The child didn't object. When they got back to Stella she was talking on her phone. She looked up from the bench, saw them approaching, said a few last words to her caller, then hung up.

"How are you feeling?" Oscar said.

"That was Harold," she said. "He wants us to come over … His mother just died."

* * *

They went straight to Harold's. He lived on the other side of Bennet Park, in an old single-family home. The place was run-down, in need of a paint job and a new roof, and the grass wanted cutting. Hanging from a pole attached to the front porch was a faded American flag.

Harold met them at the door. He was unshaven and his eyes were red, as though from crying. Moved by this, Oscar offered his condolences. Harold gave him a weak smile and thanked them for coming. Once they'd stepped into the living room, Harold turned his focus to Stella. He seemed to be trembling and looked as though he was about to start weeping.

Oscar said, "Harold, do you mind if I get Gabby a glass of water?"

"I'm not thirsty," the child said.

Oscar ignored this and looked at Harold. Harold told him where the kitchen was and Oscar led Gabby away. In the kitchen, amid a strong smell of bacon—a grease-filled pan was still on the grease-spattered stove—Oscar told his daughter to have a seat.

"You sure you don't want some water?"

"OK," she said, changing her mind.

He filled a glass from the tap and joined her at the table. In front of one of the empty chairs was a single plate, streaked with toast crumbs and dried egg yolk, and an empty coffee mug that read "World's Best Granddad." While Gabby drank from her glass Oscar watched in silence. He was wondering what the child was thinking, wondering if she was making any connections between the death of Harold's mother and the death of her own.

For Oscar, the memories were still potent, still fresh. Lila died on April 6, 2016, just after four in the morning. He had been sleeping on an air mattress in their bedroom, which he'd set up to give her more space in the bed. And for no explicable reason, he woke fully alert, overcome by a desire to check on her. He turned on a lamp and saw she was awake, and looking at him. Though by this point she had little strength, she was smiling. Oscar sat beside her and held her hand, and within minutes she was gone. Her eyes had closed and there was a peaceful look on her face.

Oscar had thought he was prepared for this moment, but he wasn't. He didn't groan or cry out but the pain was crushing, a feeling like his heart had been torn in two. Tears burned in his eyes and spilled down his cheeks. He moved closer and lay beside her, holding her over the covers, his face touching hers.

At some point Gabby came into the room. Lila had already explained to her that she was going to die, that she would be going away and they wouldn't see each other for a while. Maybe a long time. But someday they would see each other in heaven, she said, and they would be very happy. Gabby, of course, didn't fully understand—she was four years old. And when Oscar saw the child, standing by the bed, watching her parents, one living and one dead, he nearly broke down. In the several months prior to this he had told himself not to cry in front of her. Gabby had seen her mother weaken and decline, and he wanted her to know that it wasn't going to happen to him. He wanted her to know that he was strong, that he would be there for her, that she was safe and would be taken care of. So he had kept all emotion in check. And he did so now.

Rising up from the bed, he put his feet on the floor but remained seated on the mattress. His impulse was to shield the child from her mother's corpse, but part of him knew this was futile. Regardless, Gabby sidestepped him and went up to the edge of the bed, her eager eyes searching for Mommy. It was as though she knew something had happened. Oscar placed a hand on her little shoulder, to prepare her.

"Is Mommy dead?"

The breath seemed to rush from Oscar's body, as though he'd been struck. "Yes." He leaned over and took the girl into his arms, holding her. All the while she kept looking with curiosity at her mother.

Gabby didn't cry. Instead she said, "Are you going to call the doctor?"

"No, bunny."

"Why?"

"Because Mommy's dead."

"But he can make her better."

Oscar had to close his eyes. He held Gabby tight. Then he called Duncan and asked him to come get the child. He didn't want her around when the strangers arrived, the men who would take Lila's body away. For days and weeks and even months after this the two of them talked about death and how Mommy was now in heaven and wouldn't be coming back to their house. There were times, beginning with the wake and the funeral, when the finality of the situation began to sink in, that Gabby wept. But mostly the child just became sad and withdrawn, some part of her dying along with her mother. Oscar wasn't sure how to handle this. He was at a loss. He called people for advice—some of Lila's colleagues and also Lila's mother—but in the end what he did was simply to talk and spend time with Gabby. The nightly routine was strictly maintained. Oscar drove the child to school and picked her up afterward. He had her "help" with the restoration of the motorcycle. He gave her chores to do around the house. He took her to church every Sunday. They made drawings together and he bought her a dog.

Now, seated at Harold's kitchen table, Gabby said, "What are we doing?"

"We're giving Harold and Grammy some time together."

"Where's his mother?"

"I don't know. I'm guessing in this house."

Gabby lowered her eyes.

"Are you OK?"

She nodded.

"Are you sure?"

With a look of understanding, a look that was beyond her years, the child said, "Yes."

Oscar pushed back his chair and said, "Come here." He patted his thigh and Gabby came over. He lifted her onto his lap and hugged her close, enveloping her fragile body in his. He kissed her on the head and said, "I love you bunny. For ever and ever."

* * *

When he returned to the living room, Oscar found Harold and Stella seated on the sofa. Harold was resting his head on Stella's shoulder while she, looking stiff and uncomfortable, had a single hand placed on his back.

"Harold, are your kids nearby?"

Harold looked at Oscar. "No. One's in Maine, another's up in Conway, and the other's out in Las Vegas. I'll call them later."

After a pause, Oscar said, "And is ... your mother here?"

Harold nodded. Then, without a word, he stood, walked down a short hallway, opened a door, and turned back to Oscar, as though inviting him to follow. Oscar asked Stella to go sit with Gabby in the kitchen, then he and Harold went into the room and shut the door.

Harold's mother lay in bed, on her back and under the covers. Her eyes were shut and her mouth was cracked open. To Oscar it looked as though she might be asleep. He vacillated, then said, "Would you mind if I checked for a pulse?"

Harold shook his head.

Oscar lifted the woman's frail wrist and gently pressed his thumb against the veins on the underside. The wrist was cool and there was no movement. Carefully he placed the arm back by her side.

"What happened?"

Harold said when he got up that morning he had checked on her and thought she was still sleeping, so he made himself breakfast. Afterward he checked on her again and realized something was wrong. "She wasn't breathing. She was just like this."

Oscar was going to suggest they call the police, but then he noticed the crucifix above the bed. "Are you religious, Harold?"

"No ... Not since Father Seward. I stopped after that." Father Seward was the pedophile priest who had been removed from Sacred Heart ten years earlier.

"So you were Catholic?"

He nodded.

"And what about your mother?"

Another nod. "She watched Mass on TV. Even during the week. And she was always saying her rosary."

"OK. What I'm thinking, Harold, is that she would probably want a priest here right now, to say some prayers. I know a good one. He's a humble man and very devout. If you want, I could call him."

Harold looked at his mother, his eyes reddening. "She would like that."

With his phone Oscar looked up the rectory at Sacred Heart, got the number, and made the call. Father Butler himself answered. Oscar explained the situation and the priest asked for the address. After he hung up Oscar said, "He's on his way."

In a quavering voice Harold thanked Oscar.

Then Oscar said, "Harold, would you mind if I said some prayers?"

The tears streaked down Harold's face. He shook his head.

Oscar knelt beside the bed, made the sign of the cross, and began. At first he prayed internally, asking God to have mercy on this woman's soul and to help her in the transition from this world to the next. And he asked that Christ be with Harold during this difficult time. Then he prayed aloud, saying, "Our Father, Who art in heaven, hallowed be—" Abruptly he stopped, feeling a touch on his shoulder.

With some effort Harold knelt beside Oscar on the floor. He made the sign of the cross, looked at Oscar, and together the two of them started from the top.

FIFTEEN

"Hey Duncan."

"Hey Oscar."

The brothers were back at Perilloux Field. It was Vinny's Lube and Oil Change's last game of the season. Oscar had been the first to arrive, and now Duncan sat beside him in the bleachers.

"How've you been?" Oscar said.

"Eh," Duncan said with a gloomy look, and he left it at that.

They both watched the field. The coach from Hollywood Hair Salon, today's opponent, was hitting grounders to her team and barking out instructions. "Keep your eye on the ball, Katie … Thatta girl!"

"Hey, thanks again for the cookout," Oscar said. "It was a good time." A good time, he thought, except for the forty-minute speech and Bonnie telling Harold he was fat.

"I'm glad someone enjoyed themself."

"What do you mean?"

With a sad, demoralized look, Duncan shook his head.

"What?" Oscar said.

"It's Margot … She dumped me."

"Again?"

This got a sharp look from Duncan, but it was brief. He focused back on the field, and his gloomy expression returned. "Yes."

"What happened?"

"I don't know … I think it was DeProost."

"DeProost?"

"One of my assistants. You met him."

"Right."

"After my speech, I couldn't find her. So I sent him after her. He caught her leaving the house and tried to get her to come back, but evidently that didn't go so well. I called her but she didn't pick up. Then I called her the next day and we talked. I said, 'What happened?' She said, 'It was a long day. I wanted to go home.' I said, 'When can I see you again?' She said, 'Probably never.' I said, '*Probably never?*' It hurt, Oscar. It really hurt."

"I'm sorry Duncan."

"And then she said, 'You knew that I came to the party to see Oscar.' Can you believe that? Now, it was to apologize, right? Why she wanted to see you? I mean, there's nothing going on between you?"

"Uh … no. There isn't."

"I didn't think so. And no offense. It's just … she's of a different class. Very refined. The thing with her is, she's very outgoing, very friendly—with everyone. People can misinterpret that. Anyway, it looks like I'm back on the market … Again." There was frustration on his face, and pain. And then, in a rush of feeling, he said, "Why is it so hard to find love, you know? *Why?*"

Oscar felt for his brother. "Maybe she just wasn't the right fit for you."

"*The right fit*," Duncan snarled. "Was Madeline the right fit? Was Charlene?" Madeline was his first wife; Charlene his second. "I'm fit-less, Oscar. That's the problem. I'm fit-less."

"You're not fit-less. You're … You're …" Oscar drew a blank.

"I'm telling you, Margot was special. When you're rich, when you're successful, when you've achieved a certain level of prominence—it's hard to know who to trust, and I trusted her completely. She's the best damn woman I ever met."

* * *

In their orange and white uniforms the girls from Vinny's Lube and Oil Change ran onto the field and took their positions. The first Hollywood Hair Salon batter approached the plate and the umpire yelled "Play ball!" The game was on.

"How's Ma?" Duncan said, bristling with animosity.

"She's OK."

"She heckled me the other night. In front of my entire management team. *And* their families."

"I know."

"Some people laughed. I saw it. People whose lives I support. People whose lives I've supported for *years*."

"Yeah, that was … unfortunate."

"You know how much I've done for her over the years? For Ma? More than you know, Oscar, let's put it that way. More than *anybody* knows."

"Yes."

"What did we do to deserve her?"

Oscar shrugged. "Who knows? What do we do to deserve anything? You don't pick your parents."

"All my life I just wanted a normal mother. A normal family. A family like other people."

"Yeah. Me too ... Though I think a lot of people say that."

"What do you mean?"

"I mean, I think a 'happy family' is the exception, not the rule."

"Why are you sticking up for her?" Duncan said, growing suddenly fierce.

"I'm not sticking up for her," Oscar said calmly. "I admit, growing up ... it wasn't ideal. Why do you think I left? I couldn't wait to get out of Beauville. But maybe she did the best she could."

"Yeah, and maybe she didn't. In fact, maybe she didn't even try. Did you ever think of that?"

Again Oscar shrugged.

"It's true Oscar. She just didn't give a shit."

"Look, she had it tough too, growing up. A lot worse than us. We got lucky. Good teachers, good schools, good coaches. We both made it to college. For her, it was never an option. It was straight to the tannery. And who can say what was in her heart? What she was going through, why she did what she did? Dad died, and she was alone, with two kids to raise, and working in a grocery store. That would be hard for anyone. Especially someone with her background. And the memories aren't *all* bad, right? Christmases were fun. She got us presents. And she remembered our birthdays ... most of the time."

"It was easier for you," Duncan said. "You were eight when Dad died. I had to grow up fast. I had to be the responsible one.

She made me get a paper route, at ten years old. And she took all the money. Every cent! And meanwhile you were in your room, drawing all the time."

"I worked. Mowing lawns, shoveling driveways."

"Yeah, when you were older—twelve, thirteen, fourteen. I had jobs the whole time, washing dishes at the Blue Blazer, flipping burgers at McDonald's, painting houses in the summer, all while you were off drawing and playing sports."

"That's true. But you liked the money. I had other interests."

This only inflamed Duncan. "You could afford to have other interests because it was *me* who was paying for groceries!"

"What is this?" Oscar shot back. "Are you mad at *me* now?"

"No. But what I'm saying is that it was different for us. Ma dumped everything on me. You got a free ride. It's because she liked you better."

"Come on."

"*What?*"

"What the hell is this? If you're mad at her, be mad at her, don't be mad at me."

Scowling, Duncan waved a dismissive hand.

"She's the only mother we got, Duncan."

"Yeah, that's the problem. For years I waited for her to change. To be like other mothers. To be the mother I wanted. It never happened."

"Well ... I've noticed a change. She's mellowed."

"*Mellowed?*"

"Yeah. She's ... gentler. Less prickly. For the most part. And she's very good with Gabby. And you know, she has her ... charming side."

Duncan was incredulous. "*Charming side?*"

"In her own way, yeah. The thing with the two of you is that you both come out guns blazing. You expect friction, and that's exactly what you get. Maybe if you just held off on your temper, the two of you could talk."

"*Me?* She's the one who's always coming out with the insults! The wisecracks! What did I ever do to her?"

"She says you're embarrassed of her, and that you always have been. She said you sent her up to Wickham Hill not to help her but to get rid of her."

"That's bullshit," Duncan said, though with little conviction.

"And at your cookout, you refused to talk to her or even say hello. And you sent DePaul or whatever his name was—"

"DeProost."

"You sent DeProost to tell her and Harold to stay in the kitchen. How do you think that felt, being humiliated in front of strangers by her own son?"

Duncan looked out onto the field. "I knew you were taking her side."

"I'm not. I'm just saying these things are complicated. And maybe, maybe the way to go is … to just forgive her. It would be a start."

* * *

The next day, in the locker room at the Y, Oscar found Walter ranting to the hoops crew. The guys were changing into shorts and T-shirts, getting ready for b-ball combat. Already dressed in his Celtics jersey and "The Banger" headband, Walter was filling the cramped space with his bilious bluster: "I'll show that little bastard what a predator is," he was saying. "Him *and* the rest of those Facebook dingleberries."

There was laughter at this and Walter beamed. And seeing Oscar enter the room, he bellowed, "Mystery solved!"

"Mystery solved?"

"Yep. The late-night window-breaker, the car-smasher, the 'sexual predator' graffiti-artiste: it was that millennial dipshit at the Brewhouse. Logan Stoltenham—'The Manager.' "

"Right," Oscar said. "The guy you called a 'pathetic eunuch.' Who would have thought he'd be mad at you?"

"Well ..." Walter said, losing some of his fire, "he deserved it. But the point is, I'm onto him."

"How'd you find out?"

"Pam."

"Pam?"

"Yeah. I always liked her. Apart from the 'melons' stuff. No bullshit with her. But yeah, she came into the store today, said the Facebook page was the last straw."

"What Facebook page?"

"Aren't you on Facebook?"

"No."

"Twitter?"

"No."

"Well, someone made an anonymous page on Facebook." Walter swiped and tapped his phone, and handed it to Oscar.

The page was titled "Walter Bang Is a Sexual Predator." It featured a recent photo of Walter behind the counter at Big Walter's Provisions, talking with someone off camera and looking very much unaware that he was being photographed. Beneath this was a post, filled with typos, that read: "Walter Bang was band [*sic*] from Beauville Brewhouse for sexually harassing one of it's [*sic*] female employees. On more than one ocassion [*sic*] Mr. Bang made derogotory [*sic*] comments about this employees [*sic*] anatomy. Beware of this monster!"

The post had gotten more than one-hundred-eighty "likes" and assorted emojis, and a slew of comments. Some of the latter read:

"What a scumbag."

"I used to go into his store but then he started to hit on me. He said we should go out for coffee sometime!"

"LOL! He hit on me too!"

"One time I was in his store and I caught him looking down my shirt. For real! I had to tie my shoelace and when I looked up he was staring at my boobs. I felt so violated!"

"Ick! Looking down a girl's shirt? So gross!!!"

A man wrote, "I knew him in junior high. He used to give me wedgies in the cafeteria and the other kids laughed at me." This got many responses:

"Sounds like a real bully."

"Someone should beat his bully ass!"

"A bully AND a pervert!"

"There's no room for hate in Beauville. This is very disturbing."

"Keep hate OUT of Beauville!"

"What an evil, despicable man!"

"Boycott Big Walter's!"

Oscar returned the phone. "Who are these people?"

"I have no idea. I recognize a couple of them, but the rest, no. It's incredible, isn't it?"

"Among other things." Oscar undid the padlock to his locker and began changing into his gym gear. "So Pam really came in, huh? On her own?"

"Yeah. We talked," Walter said. "It was good." He made a slight shrug, looking a touch uneasy.

Curious, Oscar said, "What'd you talk about?"

"Well ... I apologized. For the comments. The 'melons' stuff."

"Really," Oscar said, impressed.

"Yeah." Again Walter made a slight shrug. "It was uncalled for."

"Hm," Oscar said, watching him. "And what about the Facebook stuff?"

"She said things had gone too far, and she wanted me to know it wasn't her."

"That was decent of her."

"It was."

"Well, it must have been a shock, when she told you. Seeing your name trashed all over the internet."

"Actually, I've known for a few days."

"How?"

"Walter the third, over in Iraq. He's on Facebook and keeps in touch with his Beauville buddies. And some of my regulars, from the store, also told me about it. But no one knew who made the page, until Pam."

"And she said it was Stoltenham."

"Yep. All of it. The damage to my property and this online nonsense. She also said little Logan's been hitting on her for months. Really hard."

A puzzled look came over Oscar. "So all of this is, what— some sort of romantic gesture?"

"Looks that way. She said he's crazy. Borderline psycho."

"Borderline?" Oscar said doubtfully.

"She also said he's an MMA freak."

"Oh man. Call the cops. Do it now."

"No. That's not how I deal with things."

One of the guys, a late teen, now seated on the bench and tying up his sneaks, said, "Walter, seriously, the dude's crazy. My brother knows him and I've heard stories. You don't want to mess."

With great bravado Walter said, "Yeah, and there was a time when people said, 'You don't want to mess with The Banger.' There's no way in hell I'm going to take any shit from some bed-wetting snowflake—MMA or no MMA."

* * *

After basketball Oscar and Walter left the Y on foot, heading for Froggie's. But on the way Walter said he wanted to make a quick detour. As they cut down Congress Street in the direction of the Brewhouse, he reached into his gym bag and put on his "The Banger" headband. It was done not with winking irony but with steely resolve, as if he were tapping into some primordial warrior instinct—an Apache brave applying his war paint, or a samurai donning his battle helmet.

"Walter, this isn't a good idea."

"I'm just going to talk to him. That's all. Put a little fright in him."

Outside the Brewhouse, Oscar stopped on the sidewalk. "Have fun."

"You're not coming in?"

"I'll read about it in the paper."

"Well, I'll just be a couple minutes."

Walter went inside, then promptly returned—followed by Logan Stoltenham.

"What are you doing?" Oscar said.

"Little Logan here asked me to 'step outside.' Apparently he's seen a few movies."

Logan appeared all business—his jaw clenched tight and his eyes focused determinedly on Walter. The kid didn't even glance at Oscar. Between the Brewhouse and the sidewalk was a brick patio used for warm-weather dining. Tonight, with dusk still an hour away, the place was packed, people eating and talking and enjoying themselves. Amid this convivial scene Walter turned to face Logan. Just perceptibly, the Manager squared up, as if readying himself for combat.

Still holding his gym bag, Walter said, "Look kid, I don't want to hurt you. But if you *ever*—"

There was a flash of movement. Quick as lightning, Logan spun around in the air—three-hundred-and-sixty degrees—and unleashed a foot to the side of Walter's head. A helicopter kick. There was a loud, bone-crunching *thwak!* Walter's body went limp and he dropped ass-backward like a felled tree. His head hit the patio floor with a brutal smack. A woman screamed. Men who had been eating shot to their feet, watching.

Logan stepped over Walter, spat on him, and, without a word, went back into the restaurant.

Oscar rushed to his friend. Flat on his back and bleeding from his nose, Walter appeared conscious but was completely out of it —his eyes open, but eerily vacant. Then, from this supine position, he began throwing harmless punches straight up into the air, like a crazy drunk flailing at ghosts.

"Hey, Walter—Walter!" Oscar said, now on his knees, trying to calm him.

A crowd gathered around them and a woman said, "Should I call an ambulance?"

Another woman said, "Isn't that the guy on Facebook?"

"Walter, it's OK," Oscar said, as Walter continued to throw his feeble fists at a nonexistent opponent. Oscar grabbed both of Walter's hands and brought them down to his stomach. Walter's resistance lessened. His eyes were still dazed, but slowly, slowly, he seemed to come to.

Out of the Brewhouse came Pam. Seeing Walter laid out on the ground she shook her head, looking both annoyed and concerned, and walked over.

In a groggy voice, Walter greeted her: "Hi Pam."

She ignored this and instead addressed Oscar. "Is he all right?"

"I think so."

"Has anyone called the cops?" No one had, so she pulled a phone from her waitress apron and dialed 911.

* * *

By the time the police cruiser arrived, lights flashing but no siren, Walter was sitting up and holding a paper napkin to this nose.

"Is that you Walter?" said the elder of the two cops. His tone was informal and familiar, and his nametag read "Sgt. Flick."

Still wearing his "The Banger" headband, Walter said, "Yep. It's me." His tone also was informal and familiar, and Oscar wasn't surprised. As his father had done before him, Walter provided free coffee to the boys in blue on their regular stops at Big Walter's Provisions. Because of this multi-generational generosity, the store had attained a special, even legendary status at Beauville Police Headquarters. Seasoned cops would bring rookies into the store over their first weeks for a meet and greet with the popular proprietor.

"Looks like you got your ass kicked," Sergeant Flick said.

"More like my face," Walter said.

"What happened?"

"Some sort of karate kick. I didn't see it coming."

"No, I mean—what caused it?"

"Oh. I figured out who busted up my store, and my car."

"Who?"

"A kid who works here."

"And he did this to you?"

Embarrassed, humbled, Walter nodded. "Yeah."

Sergeant Flick looked to his partner, then motioned his head toward the Brewhouse entrance as if to say, "Go get him."

But that wasn't necessary. For just then Logan Stoltenham came onto the patio.

"Unbelievable," Sergeant Flick said, as though he was well acquainted with Stoltenham and was neither surprised nor pleased to see him.

Stoltenham pointed at Walter. "This gentleman has been sexually harassing my waitstaff, and this evening he came in making threats. To protect the restaurant, and myself, I took the necessary measures. It was self-defense. I know my rights!"

"I never threatened you," Walter grumbled, still sitting on the ground. "And I never sexually harassed his waitstaff," he added, now looking up at Sergeant Flick.

Aware that all attention had now shifted to him, Sergeant Flick sagaciously pursed his lips and assumed a weighty, authoritative air. He looked over the crowd, sniffed in some clean Beauville air, then hitched up his pants. Finally he said, "Who saw what happened?"

Several people held up a hand, including Oscar and the woman who had screamed. Statements were taken and soon afterward Stoltenham was cuffed and led off to the cruiser.

By now Walter had gotten to his feet. Sergeant Flick encouraged him to go to the hospital—if not for health reasons, he said, then at least for legal ones—but Walter refused. "I'm fine," he said. But when the sergeant asked if he wanted to press charges, Walter frowned. In his worldview, pressing charges was for pussies. And Walter Bang was no pussy. Yet now, he wavered. And the longer he did, the more dejected he appeared. At last, in a bleak, doleful voice, he said, "Yeah. I suppose I will."

SIXTEEN

Days later Oscar drove Harold to Beauville Hospital. Since his mother's death, Harold had been in a bad way. At the wake, surrounded by his children and grandchildren, his VFW buddies and his bowling team, he had broken down and wept. At the funeral Mass and burial, and the reception afterward at the Beauville VFW Hall, he had appeared pale and shaken, haggard and withdrawn. Because Harold was now alone, Oscar told Stella she could invite him over anytime. Harold came for supper four nights in a row, and during their most recent meal, while they all sat at the picnic table in the backyard, he groaned and reached for his chest.

At the ER, Oscar gave the admitting nurse Harold's symptoms, including the recent stress and depression caused by his mother's death. Harold was immediately taken in. An hour later another nurse came to the waiting room to say they would be keeping him overnight. Stella was then allowed to go sit with the patient.

Afterward, on the walk out to the car, she was quiet.

"Is Harold OK?" Gabby said.

"We'll see," Stella said.

* * *

The next day around noon, the three Perillouxs drove back to the hospital. Stella sat silent in the passenger seat, pensive and grim. In the backseat Gabby likewise was silent, the child gazing glumly out the window. The evening before, during their nightly tuck-in, she had asked Oscar if Harold was going to die. "I don't know," he had said. "Let's pray that he gets better." And so they did. Afterward she said, "If he dies will he be with Mommy?" Oscar said, "Yes."

At the information desk they learned that Harold was still on the emergency wing, but now in a private room. They went down several corridors, through two sets of pneumatic doors, got lost once, then finally found the room. Oscar knocked at the door and was told to come in.

Sitting up in bed, and dressed in a light-blue johnny, Harold was holding a sandwich and chewing. A lunch tray was set before him, and on the wall opposite him a television blared. Two talking heads were shouting at each other, something about Tom Brady and the Patriots.

"Hey, Oscar! Come on in!" Harold said.

Oscar was dumbfounded. He had expected the worst: Harold on life support; Harold struggling for survival; Harold a near-corpse. But Harold was very much alive, his eyes happy and bright.

"You don't look dead," Stella said, coming in behind Oscar.

Harold's gaze locked on hers and his face shined.

Next came Gabby. Immediately she beamed, her little face elated, as she sensed from the smiles and the voices of the adults that everything was all right.

"No, I'm not dead," Harold said. "Not yet." He explained that all his tests had come back negative for a heart attack. "They think it was just anxiety."

"That's great Harold," Oscar said. "Wonderful news."

Stella said nothing, but from her expression it was plain she was relieved, and moved. The worry and fear of the past two days were gone.

Harold put down the remains of his sandwich, wiped his hands on a napkin, and turned off the TV. Then, like a gentleman of old, a knight requesting a dance with his beloved lady, he extended a hand to Stella. She tried to frown, to express her disapproval, but her happy eyes betrayed her true feelings. Stepping close to the bed, she took his hand in hers. Neither of them spoke. Words were not necessary.

Touched by this—the tenderness, and even somehow the innocence—Oscar averted his gaze. Gabby was less restrained. Like Stella on the sofa watching *Restless Hearts*, the child was engrossed, staring raptly at the scene playing before her.

Presently Oscar said, "So how was your night, Harold?"

"One of the worst of my life," he said. "I thought I was going to die. I'd never had chest pains like that before. I was so scared I couldn't sleep, and then when I finally started to, someone came in to draw blood. Every three hours they did it—someone would come in and jab a needle in my arm. It was awful. But then this morning they did more tests and said everything looked fine. I was so happy." He looked at Stella and his eyes became red. "I'm not ready to die. There are still some things I want to do."

Again Oscar averted his gaze. And again Gabby stared.

Harold said, "Gabby, would you grab my pants? They're in the bag there." He pointed to a stuffed plastic bag, filled with his clothes, that had been set on a chair beneath the television. Gabby did as he asked, then Harold went into the back pocket of his blue jeans and pulled out an old nylon wallet with frayed edges. "I'm sorry," he said, "but this can't wait."

Pushing away the portable food tray, he tossed aside his blanket, swung his hairy legs over the edge of the bed, planted his bare feet on the floor, and stood with some effort. The three Perillouxs watched, and wondered.

With a loud ripping sound, Harold opened one of the wallet's Velcro pockets and extracted a ring—a diamond ring.

Gabby gasped.

Oscar's eyebrows shot up.

Stella, who had backed into a corner, seemed completely unfazed.

Harold turned to face her. Then, swiveling his head back, he said, "Oscar, give me a hand."

Oscar stepped forward and helped lower Harold down to one knee. What Harold may or may not have known was that much of his person was now exposed to Oscar and Gabby, who stood behind him. The johnny covered Harold's front and sides but left open all of the back, head to foot. Mercifully, he was wearing his Fruit of the Looms.

Gabby missed none of this. Despite her young age, she sensed the humor of the situation, and looked up at her father with a secret, mirthful smile. Oscar gave her a discreet wink.

From his knee, Harold was gazing up at the object of his enduring love. He said, "Stella, you've always been in my heart.

When we were in high school, and I was on the football field or in the classroom, you were in my heart. When I was overseas and getting shot at and laid up in a hospital, you were in my heart. When I got married and had a family, and Ellie and the kids were in my heart, you were still in there too. And you've been in there all the years since, and for seven years now I've been carrying this ring around waiting for the day I could give it to you. And last night ..." He choked up, his voice trembling. "And last night, I prayed to God not to let me die. I don't want to lose you Stella. Not again. I want you to be my wife."

From Stella's glistening eyes a tear rolled down her cheek. Then another tear came, and then another.

* * *

With their backs against the headboard, Oscar and Gabby were sitting up in the child's bed. They had just finished the evening prayer, and now Oscar was going to read aloud from their current book, a kids' version of *Oliver Twist*. Quite frankly, Oscar was looking forward to it. Not just for the story—which he was enjoying—but for the welcome return to routine following what had been a tumultuous few days. First there had been the trips to the hospital and the specter of Harold's death. Next came the bombshell of his mother's engagement. And earlier, over supper, there had been an unsettling exchange with Gabby. The two of them were alone, as Stella had decided to spend the night at Harold's. Eating her veggie chili, the child had been unusually quiet, looking as though she was contemplating some great question. Then, at last, she said, "Am *I* going to get married?"

Caught off guard by this, Oscar had said, "Well ... sure. Some day. If you want to." Gabby nodded, then resumed her ponderous silence, her mind still turning things over. At this, Oscar had felt a twinge of alarm. The idea of his daughter entering the realm of romantic relations was not something he wanted to think about. Not yet. Maybe in, oh, ten, fifteen years. Now, however, book in hand, and with the girl safely at his side, all seemed right in Oscar's world. Order had been restored. Normalcy resumed.

He opened *Oliver Twist* to where they had left off the night before, cleared his throat, and was about to begin when Gabby spoke up.

"Daddy, what was I like when I was little?"

"*What?*"

She was looking across the room, at the framed photo hanging above the fish tank. It was a black-and-white image, taken on a rooftop in Brooklyn. In it, Lila holds three-year-old Gabby as the two of them laugh, their eyes shining with joy, shining with life. At the time, the three of them had already moved to New Hampshire and were back in the city visiting friends.

"When I was little, what was I like?"

"You mean, when you were littler than you are now?"

"I'm not little. I'm eight years old."

Oscar fidgeted slightly. "Yes ... Well, when you were *really* little, you were very happy. You smiled a lot. People always used to say that. You were a happy baby."

"That's good."

"It is."

"And how did I talk?"

"Uh, let's see … You used to say 'app-oh' for apple. That was funny."

The child giggled. "App-oh?"

"Yep."

"I don't remember that. What else?"

"You used to say 'glubs' for gloves, and 'dint' for didn't. Mommy took care of that."

Another giggle.

"Why do you ask?"

"I don't know. I was just wondering. But Dad?"

"Yeah?"

"I can read by myself."

"What?"

"I can read my own book now."

Oscar looked at her. Then he understood. "Oh."

"If you want, you can read your own book too."

This Oscar also understood. Gabby was saying that, if he didn't want to leave, he could get another book and read here beside her. "I think I'm all set," he said, suddenly feeling a bit awkward.

The child just nodded, and the two of them looked at each other.

"Well … I guess I'll get ready for bed," Oscar said.

"OK."

He handed her the book, gave her a kiss, told her he loved her, then said goodnight.

* * *

Up in his studio/bedroom Oscar struck a match. He lit a votive candle, set it within a red-glass candleholder, and placed it atop the small bookcase he was using as a temporary altar. Above this and hanging from the wall was an icon of Christ, which he had taken from his old room before his mother had moved in. Lila had bought the icon at a church in Manhattan, the Shrine of the Holy Innocents, and now it was one of Oscar's most precious possessions. Morning and night, in the years leading up to her death, Lila would light a candle, kneel before the icon, and pray for fifteen, twenty minutes at a time. After she died, Oscar started to do the same.

Turning off the electric light, he took his position in front of the icon and knelt on a cushion on the floor. Instantly, a feeling of comfort passed over him. A feeling of security, a feeling of hope. For here, in this space, was truth, and beauty. The silence and the stillness. The soft glow of the flame. The ancient image of Christ dimly visible in the golden light. In this way, in this setting, Oscar connected with God. God the creator of all things. God who was patient and all-loving. God the great mystery. God the eternal light.

Often during these nightly sessions Oscar would meditate on Christ and pray in his mind, conversationally, rather than through the recitation of formal words. Tonight was no different. He crossed himself and began. First he thought about Gabby. He was pondering what she had just said to him: "I can read my own book now." Oscar smiled but also felt a pang, as the comment was yet another reminder that the child was growing up. The memory of her birth—thirty hours of labor, and much suffering for Lila—was still fresh to him, still real. Yet this fall Gabby would be in the third grade. These were the precious years, the formative years, the years of unquestioning love, and already they were slipping away. Oscar prayed to Christ for His help, that He continue to guide him as a parent, and that He bless and protect Gabby in all things. Next Oscar wondered about himself. How was he doing? As a father? As a son? As a brother? As a friend? In each case the answer was, as always: he could do better. Oscar asked that Christ have mercy on him, and that He give him the grace and the strength and the courage to be better. A better father, a better son, a better brother, a better friend, a better person. More loving, more forgiving, more merciful, more humble. Then Oscar prayed for his people, both the living and the dead. He prayed for Lila and for Stella. For his father and for Harold. For Duncan and his children. For Walter and his family ... And he prayed too for Margot and her little ones.

As usual, the thought of Margot provoked some inner excitement. A quickening of the pulse, a stirring of the mind. Focusing on the icon in the golden light, observing Christ with his inscrutable gaze, Oscar realized it was time. In the weeks before she died, Lila had wanted Oscar to promise her two things. One, that he would continue to take Gabby to church after she was gone. And two, that he would remarry. Oscar had agreed to the first but had held off on the second. The thought of it seemed obscene—not to mention inconceivable. How could there be another? It was impossible. It could never be. But things had changed. He had loved Lila, and always would. But the same heart that loved her was now longing for Margot.

* * *

Late the next morning the doorbell rang, sending Mindy into an obligatory fit of barking. Paint brush in hand, Oscar had been concentrating on his canvas; now, he was wondering if any of his neighbors might want a new dog. He was in his studio, going over another of his abandoned-quarry paintings. The first one had come out so well that he had decided to do a series. He would do five or six paintings of the same quarry from different perspectives, focusing on different elements, different forms. He gave the painting a quick last look, set his brush on the palette, removed his vinyl gloves, and went down to the living room. He shushed the dog but of course she kept barking. He told Gabby to take her out to the backyard, then went down to the front door.

Stella and Harold stood on the porch. Harold was grinning, his red face blooming. Stella, though less buoyant, also looked happy.

"Well," Oscar said archly, "you guys have a good night?"

Still grinning, Harold seemed to blush—though given his cheeks normal red hue it was difficult to tell for sure. Stella was less amused.

Harold said, "We went to the Millstone for supper—they do a nice early bird special. I had the prime rib and your mother had the chicken cordon bleu. The prime rib was a touch overcooked, but all in all it was a good meal. After that we drove to the lake to get some ice cream, and then, well …"

"It's none of your business," Stella said, finishing the sentence.

"Understood," Oscar said.

As they went up to the living room Stella announced that she had come to get her things. "I'm moving in with Harold," she said.

"That was fast," Oscar said.

"We don't want to waste any time," Harold said. "Life is short."

"That it is," Oscar said, though his thoughts were concentrated less on the brevity of earthly existence and more on how Stella had agreed to watch Gabby this summer. Apparently that deal was now off.

"Hi Grammy!" Gabby said, coming into the room. She went straight over to Stella and gave her a hug. Oscar paid special attention. Part of him, call it the cynical part, was wondering if his mother might be indifferent to the child—or worse—now that she had a better living arrangement.

But Stella surprised. As Gabby wrapped her arms around her waist, Stella smiled and returned the hug, her expression natural and warm. "How are you sweetie?" she said.

Oscar was impressed.

"Do you want to go to the park?" the child said.

"No, I can't. Not today."

"Why?"

"Because today I'm moving into Harold's house."

"You are?"

"Yep."

"Why?"

"Because we're getting married."

"But aren't you taking care of me this summer?"

There was a long pause.

Harold looked uneasy.

Oscar waited.

At last Stella said, "Yes ... Three days a week I'll come over. Till you go back to school." Though the words were said to Gabby, they seemed equally addressed to Oscar.

To him, it seemed like a fair deal. Maybe even more than a fair deal. He asked them to stay for lunch.

"Sounds good," Harold said, pleased by the idea.

Stella seemed pleased too.

* * *

They were out on the back deck, eating at the table. Oscar had made sandwiches and filled a bowl with chips.

"So what are your plans?" he said.

"We're going to do the deed at City Hall," Harold said. "Then maybe have a reception down to the VFW."

"What's 'the deed'?" Gabby said.

"Getting married," Stella said.

"At church?" Gabby said.

"No. City Hall."

"What's that?"

"It's a government place. Where the mayor is. People like that."

Gabby looked confused.

"People get married there too, not just at church," Oscar said.

Gabby looked at Stella.

"I'd need an annulment for a church wedding," she said. "Among other things."

"I could make a call," Oscar said.

"Nah," she said. "I don't believe in that stuff."

Oscar winced, and reflexively scratched his cheek with his left hand. As he did this, Stella's eyes narrowed and her brow creased. Oscar thought she had gotten huffy and was giving him a reproachful look. But then he realized the keen-eyed woman had in fact noticed the change: last night, after his prayers, Oscar had removed his wedding band. With some sadness and even some guilt, he had slid the ring off, kissed it, then set it next to the flickering candle, in front of the icon. Lowering his hand now, he made no comment to his mother. Instead he turned to Harold and said, "And when is all this going to happen?"

"Probably next week. I'm going over to the VFW today."

"Why don't you have it here?"

"What?"

"Everything. The wedding, the reception. We could do it in the yard."

SEVENTEEN

"Hello?"

"Hey Margot—it's Oscar."

"Hi, how are you?"

"Good, good. How are things?"

"They're good."

"And the kids?"

"Oh, they're great. Having fun up here at the lake."

"Oh, that's good … So you guys are still up there."

"Yeah. Probably till September."

"OK. Excellent … So, uh, the reason I'm calling is, I wanted to invite you to my mother's wedding."

There was silence. Then: "Your mother?"

"Yes. She's marrying Harold. You met him."

"Yes, I remember … Oh, that's wonderful. Good for them."

More silence.

"Hello?" Oscar said.

"Yes, I'm here … And when is it?"

"Not this Saturday, but next Saturday. It's at my house. Zora and Sana are invited too, of course. Gabby will be thrilled to see them."

"And is, uh … Duncan going too? … And Bonnie?"

"Well, I'm not sure. I haven't called him yet. There's some friction between him and my mother. It's a long story. But my guess is he won't come."

"Actually, I'm sorry. I shouldn't have asked. It's none of my business."

"No, it's fine. I understand. So what do you say?"

"Mmm … Well … OK. Yeah, I'll go. It sounds like fun."

* * *

That Saturday, the Saturday before the wedding, Oscar got a text. Margot wrote: "Are you going to be home today? Around three?"

Oscar replied "Yes," and later, around three, his doorbell rang.

He had already tidied up the house, brought the dog outside, and put on a clean shirt. With his heart thumping—more from joy than nerves—he went downstairs to let her in.

At the door she met him with a smile. It was the smile he now carried around in his mind, the smile he remembered when he thought of her: warm, playful, and ever ready to break into merry laughter at the least hint of the comic or the ridiculous.

He said hello and noted that she was lightly tanned, her olive complexion glowing with a golden, brownish tint. She wore a sleeveless sundress with simple leather sandals and was holding a handbag and also a shop bag.

Oscar invited her in, then hesitated. Should he let her go up the stairs first, or should he? If he went first, it might seem rude. But if he encouraged her to go first, she might think he was using the opportunity to check out her bottom and her legs—which might possibly be the case.

Margot herself resolved the dilemma. She simply started up the stairs, saying, "It's a beautiful day."

"Yes," Oscar said, trailing behind. "It is."

In the living room, she looked the space over. Oscar felt a prick of insecurity. The room wasn't quite as grand as Duncan's living room. In fact, Duncan's living room was probably bigger than Oscar's entire apartment. But Margot didn't seem to mind. She made a beeline for one of his paintings.

Above the sofa was a three-by-four-foot picture of birch trees and moss-covered rocks. The image was cropped, showing a close-up view of the different forms.

"Oh, it's lovely," Margot said, and for some time she studied the canvas. "New Hampshire?"

"Yes. Beauville. Out near the reservoir."

She continued to look at the painting, her eyes immersed in the scene, her attention fully absorbed. Without question, Oscar was enjoying this. It reminded him of Freud's theory about artists and their goals—namely, fame, fortune, and beautiful lovers. Like much of Freud, the idea was reductive and even silly. But in this instance …

"Hi Mrs. Saadeh!" Gabby said, coming into the room.

Margot appeared delighted to see the child, and she asked her about softball and her summer. Afterward she said, to Oscar, "So the reason I wanted to come over is that I was shopping the other day and I saw this great dress. I thought it would be perfect for Gabby. For the wedding."

Oscar hadn't thought about that—a dress for Gabby. And to be honest, he was fairly certain the child didn't even own one. Not one that still fit, anyway.

Margot took the dress out of the bag and held it up for Gabby to see. "What do you think?"

Looking the thing over, Gabby just nodded, cautiously. She seemed guarded but also potentially interested.

"Do you want me to help you try it on?" Margot said.

Again the child nodded, and she led Margot off to the bathroom. When they returned Gabby was beaming. The dress fit her perfectly, and she looked adorable, transformed. And very unexpectedly, Oscar felt a stinging in his eyes. He glanced away, blinking, wanting to stifle the emotion.

"What's wrong?" Gabby said.

"Nothing. A bug flew in my eye ... You look very pretty, bunny. Do you like it?"

Another nod, this time with enthusiasm.

"Thank you, Margot," Oscar said. He reached for his wallet and asked how much he owed her. She insisted it was a gift. "A late birthday present," she said. There were more thank-yous, including from Gabby, and after the dress had been removed and hung in a closet, the three of them were back in the living room.

Margot said, "You know, I actually happen to have my shears with me."

"Your *shears?*"

"Yes. Scissors. For cutting hair."

Oscar's brow furrowed, and a smidgen of apprehension showed on Margot's face.

"Sometimes I cut the girls' hair," she said. "And since I'm here ... If you want I could maybe give Gabby a little trim."

"You keep shears in your purse?"

"Well, now that I'm between houses ... I came down from the lake to pick up a few things. Including the shears."

"I see ..." Oscar said. He recalled, quite vividly, Margot's horror when she had first seen Gabby's hair up close, many weeks ago at the Sacred Heart coffee social. Some people might have taken offense, then and now. But not Oscar. He was happy for the help. He said, "You don't mind?"

* * *

They were still in the living room. Oscar had moved the coffee table off to the side and put in its place a kitchen chair, which Gabby now sat on. Draped around her shoulders and neck was a bath towel. Margot, focused but chatty, was snipping away with her shears. Oscar, fairly stunned that this was actually happening, sat on the sofa, watching.

"What are Zora and Sana doing today?" Gabby asked.

"Last I knew they were going for a boat ride."

"Where?"

"On Lake Winnipesaukee. Their uncle has a sailboat."

"Do they like birds?"

"Zora and Sana?"

Gabby nodded.

"Um, I think so. At the lake we have a cardinal that comes around quite a bit. That's always fun to see."

"Is it a male or a female?" the child asked.

"Uh ... I don't know."

"Is it red or brown?"

"Red."

"That's a male. And this is how they sound ..." Gabby sat up straight, and with a look of high seriousness, and not one bit of self-consciousness, she stared at Margot and whistled the call of a male cardinal: "Fweeet, fweeet, fweeet, foo-foo-foo-foo-foo ... Fweeet, fweeet, fweeet, foo-foo-foo-foo-foo ..."

Margot's laughter filled the room. "Yes, that's it. That's exactly how he sounds."

* * *

When the job was finished, the ladies went into the bathroom to have a look in the mirror. As with the dress, Gabby returned to the living room beaming.

"Very pretty," Oscar said, though he barely noticed a difference. The hair was about the same length as it was before the cut, though now somewhat neater.

But Gabby seemed to have noticed a difference. With chin raised high, she was making her proud face, her eyes sparkly with satisfaction.

"What do you say?" Oscar said.

The child thanked Margot, then went off toward her room.

"This has been great," Oscar said. "Thank you."

"We're not finished," Margot said.

Oscar's eyebrows went up, suggestively. "No?"

"No," she said, glancing at the chair. "You're next."

"Me?"

"Yes. Trust me."

Oscar felt a flicker of concern.

"Just a trim," she said. "Don't worry."

He stood and obediently sat on the chair. Margot draped the towel around his shoulders and tucked it into the neck of his jersey. As she did this, as she touched him with her hands and hovered at his side, her body close and fragrant—Oscar had caught a subtle whiff of a very pleasant perfume—he said, "*Hmm.*"

"What?"

"I was just thinking how this is better than cutting it myself."

She gave him a look, then began combing out his hair. She circled around him then came to a stop directly in front of him. Oscar wasn't sure where to fix his gaze. Her chest was at eye-level.

"Gabby's really sweet," she said, now combing his bangs. "You've done a great job with her."

"Wow ... That's a switch."

"I know. I deserve that. But it's true. I still think about the pony rides, the way she let Bonnie have her pony."

Recalling not just the pony rides but also the sleepover party that had followed, Oscar said, "Yeah, it was ... a memorable day."

Margot didn't disagree. She then took up her shears and got to work. As she cut his hair they chatted about the twins and the lake, and then about Beauville and New York, and it wasn't long before Oscar realized that he wanted to touch her. Run a hand down the side of her body. Pull her close. Plant a kiss on her lips. Something. But instead of kissing her he placed his hands flat on the tops of his thighs. It was a clumsy move. Maybe a desperate move. His way of saying, "Look—no ring!" Purposely he avoided eye contact, wanting to give her gaze the freedom to roam, wanting her to make the discovery herself, and for some time the two of them were silent. When at last he looked up, he saw that *she* was now avoiding his eye, and that her expression had tensed.

Oscar said, "So why did you leave the cookout early?"

"Duncan's cookout?"

"Yes."

"Oh, it was getting late. A long day."

"OK," Oscar said, though he wasn't convinced.

"I felt uncomfortable," Margot said.

"Because of me?"

"No. Not at all ... Other people. Duncan's assistant ... I forget his name—"

"DeProost."

"Yes, DeProost. Like de writer," she quipped. "When I first arrived he asked if I wouldn't mind standing up on the dais behind Duncan, during his speech."

Oscar laughed. "What an offer."

Now Margot laughed. "Yes. And after the speech he wouldn't let me leave. He said Duncan wanted to see me. He's very persistent, your brother."

"He is. He's a determined guy. But look at it this way: you got a free pin."

Again she laughed. "That's right: 'Making a Better World' ... Also, I have to say I was a little surprised that he wouldn't talk to your mother, in public like that. Not that it's any of my business."

"It's complicated," Oscar said, now feeling a stab of guilt, like he maybe wasn't being as loyal to his brother as he should be.

"But Duncan's been very good to her. For years he supported her. He's been very generous. He's a good man."

Margot nodded, diplomatically, and continued snipping with the shears. "I remember when she said she lived with you."

"My mother?"

"Yes. At the table. You looked embarrassed."

"Well …"

"I was actually impressed."

"By what?"

"That she lived with you."

"You were?"

"Yes. In Lebanon and the Middle East it's normal for three generations to live together, in the same house. Here people have more money and more space but they ship old people into homes. I don't understand it. It seems barbaric."

"Yeah," Oscar said, thinking back to what he had seen at Riverside Pines. He said, "Were you born there? In Lebanon?"

"No, here. But my parents were. A lot of my family left the country. Some went to France, others came here."

"Where are your parents now?"

"My mom's dead. My dad's in Delaware. My brother too."

"I'm sorry to hear that, about your mom."

"It was a long time ago. When I was in high school."

Gabby came into the room. "Daddy, can I have some ice cream?"

"No. Have a banana."

The child left, but soon returned. She sat on the sofa, peeled the banana, and took a bite. Chewing, she watched the two adults. They were silent, so she said, "I never went to a wedding before."

"No?" Margot said.

Gabby shook her head.

"Well, they're fun. You'll have a good time."

When Margot finished the haircut, Oscar inspected the results in the bathroom mirror. He thought he looked pretty good. Certainly better than he did twenty minutes earlier. "Not bad," he said, coming back into the living room. Then, with his pulse quickening, he said, "Hey, would you like to go out for supper? As a thank you? I could call for a sitter."

"Oh … I'm sorry. I can't."

"That's OK."

"Stan's coming up. My ex. He's staying at the lake for a few days, to see the girls. He should be there now."

"Ah," Oscar said. *The ex.* He was curious to know more, but he kept quiet.

"Anyway, I should go," Margot said.

"Sure."

"But I enjoyed this," she added. And smiled.

EIGHTEEN

The neck brace was making life difficult for Walter. To drink his beer, he had to lean forward and carefully tip the bottle into his mouth. But at the moment he didn't seem to mind. He was all fired up, animated and loud. Seated in a booth at Froggie's Tap Room, he was giving Oscar the latest. The list of grievances on the "Walter Bang Is a Sexual Predator" Facebook page was still growing, as was the controversy.

"I don't even know who this one is!" he said. "She claims I grabbed her ass in high school, at some party, and now she's demanding an apology! Do you remember her?"

Walter showed Oscar his phone. On the screen was the post in question along with the name and thumbnail photo of this new accuser. Oscar didn't recognize her.

"It's really incredible," Walter said. "One day I'm just a guy with a convenience store; the next, I'm an enemy of the people."

It was true. Much had happened to Walter since the appearance of the Facebook page and his one-kick knockout at the hands, or rather the foot, of Logan Stoltenham. The morning after the incident, Walter drove himself to Beauville Hospital. He had a migraine, his vision was blurry, and he couldn't move his head without shooting pain. After an examination and a CT scan, he was given the neck brace and a diagnosis of whiplash and concussion. Walter pushed ahead with criminal charges against Stoltenham and also contacted a personal injury lawyer. "I'm gonna sue the little bastard," Walter declared.

For his part, Logan Stoltenham had become a social-media star. After a night in the Beauville PD lockup, he posted bail and learned that he had been fired from the Brewhouse. But since then, he was all over the internet. A number of activists had taken up his cause, and his exploits in the "fight against hate and sexual violence" were shared and discussed on Facebook and Twitter. Celebrities of all sorts, from Hollywood stars and best-selling authors, to professional athletes and Silicon Valley moguls, praised and championed Stoltenham's courage in the crusade for social justice. This in turn led to a flurry of interest from the mainstream media. In adulatory, and even hagiographic terms, Stoltenham was written about and interviewed, the subject of countless news items, profiles, think pieces, and podcasts. There was also a Go-FundMe campaign created in support of "The Logan Stoltenham Legal Defense Fund."

"He's already up to three-hundred-and-seventy-thousand bucks," Walter said. "It's unbelievable! He's going to be rich! But that's not all. Now they're going to have a rally."

"A rally?"

Walter swiped his phone and showed Oscar. It was another Facebook page.

" 'A Protest Against Hate,' " Oscar read aloud. "Twelve-hundred-thirty-nine likes." He scrolled through the page and saw many posts of support and endless comments. "When is this?"

"Saturday," Walter said. "They're starting at City Hall and marching to Big Walter's. Then they're going to have the rally in the park across the street."

"Come on," Oscar said in disbelief.

"Yes," Walter said, grinning with roguish pleasure.

"Is it even legal?"

"Of course. They got a permit."

"You don't seem too concerned."

"Are you kidding? The store's doing great business. Better than ever. I've lost some customers, but I've gained even more. Do you know Beano? Paulie Beauchene?"

"No."

"He's one of these right-wing militia guys. Thinks George Soros and Bill Gates and all the rest of them are plotting a one-world government and are coming after his guns. He's a regular at the store, a real character. Likes to come in and bullshit and talk politics. He knows I've been a lifelong liberal, and he loves to make fun of the Teddy Kennedy picture, but he's a good guy." On the wall behind the cash register at Big Walter's was a framed but now fading color photograph of Big Walter and Senator Kennedy, who had stopped in at the store during the 1980 presidential campaign. "Anyway, Beano's setting up a counter-rally."

"A counter-rally?"

"Yeah. At Big Walter's, in the parking lot."

Trying to process this, Oscar said, "So you're going to have a rally with a right-wing militia, even though you're a lifelong liberal."

"*Was* a lifelong liberal. Those are the exact people who want to destroy me. Screw them. The virtue police. And these right-wing guys, they're my bread and butter. Most of my customers voted for Trump."

"Wow," Oscar said, mulling this and sipping his beer.

"Yeah, Big Walter's probably rolling over in his grave. We were always blue-collar liberals. You know: freedom of speech, rule of law, and sticking up for the little guy. I'll do and say what I want, and you'll do and say what you want, and so long as nobody breaks the law, everyone's happy. The American Way, right? But these idiots?" he said, holding up his phone and indicating the Facebook digital mob. "They want none of that. They want to ruin me and ruin my business. I'm telling you, it's war."

Heidi the waitress came to the table. "How you guys doin'? Another round?"

With the neck brace limiting his movement, Walter turned stiffly to see her. He said yes to the beers then added, "You coming to the rally on Saturday?"

"I think so," she said. "Billy's gotta go see his mother, she's still up the hospital, but he wants to go. I think we'll be there. I know Kenny MacLain's going, and Liz Kuhnke."

"Good. We need to fight those bastards," Walter said.

Heidi nodded and walked off.

"Are you coming?" Walter asked Oscar.

"You know, as much as I'd love to watch a bunch of lunatics yelling at each other, I actually have plans. My mother's getting married."

"What? *No.*"

"Yes."

"To Harold?"

"Yep."

"Well hey, that's great. Harold's a good guy. He comes in for a twelve pack every now and then. Real nice guy."

"Yeah. My mother got lucky."

"Well, good for her."

The new beers came. Walter took a healthy swig of his, then looked at Oscar. His eyes were shining, filled with a passionate intensity. "I have to tell you something, Oscar. Since this whole thing started, I've been feeling really good—that is, apart from the concussion and getting my ass kicked by a ninety-pound millennial. But the depression, it's gone. Completely. All these people coming into the store, saying they're behind me, supporting the rally—it's energizing. I told you before that I was looking for something. My shrink said, 'Get a dog.' I'm starting to think the answer is politics."

* * *

First thing Saturday morning eight guys and two large trucks arrived at Oscar's place. They had come to set up a tent, lay down a dancefloor, and wire up a PA system. The previous day a landscaping crew had cut the lawn, trimmed the bushes, and raked up all the dog shit. Around ten a.m. the caterers were expected. All of this, including the DJ who was expected around noon, was paid for by Duncan.

Initially, Stella hadn't wanted to invite him. "To hell with Duncan!" she had said. "He can go to my funeral." But Harold thought this wrong. "He's your son, Stell. Let bygones be bygones." Oscar, for reasons of his own, had stayed out of it. Then, about a week ago, Stella relented. She told Oscar, "Go ahead and invite him. But tell him to keep that Bonnie on a short leash. Any crap from either one of them and I'll kick 'em both out myself." So Oscar made the call.

Not surprisingly, Duncan showed little interest in attending. "I'm busy on Saturday," he said. "A business thing. But we'll see. Maybe I'll stop by. Who else is going?"

At this, Oscar felt conscience-bound to admit that Margot would be there.

"*Margot?*" Duncan cried. "Is there something going on between you two?"

To be honest, Oscar didn't know if there was something going on between them. Certainly, *he* had feelings for her. But where she stood, he couldn't say. So he said, "She hit it off with Ma and Harold at your Fourth of July cookout, and Harold wanted to invite her." This was all true. Harold *had* wanted to invite Margot, and he had been the first to suggest the idea to Oscar.

"Oh, OK. Yeah, she's like that," Duncan said. "I told you before that she was overfriendly to people. Well, yeah, I'll come. Where is it?"

Oscar told him.

"*Your* place?" Duncan said. "What is this going to be, burgers and dogs on the grill?"

"Something like that," Oscar said.

"No, no, no. It's too embarrassing. Look, I'll take care of this." And so he did.

* * *

When Gabby came into the kitchen that morning she was already in her new dress. Oscar was at the counter making coffee.

"Bunny, people aren't coming till two."

"That's OK."

"What I mean is, you might get food on your dress. You should put it on after lunch."

"But I want to wear it now."

"OK," he said.

"Where's Mindy?"

"She's in my room. I don't want her barking at the guys putting up the tent."

"Can I watch them?"

"Sure. We'll have breakfast out on the deck."

* * *

Around noon the doorbell rang. Oscar, back again in his old bedroom, was getting into his one and only suit. Over Mindy's delirious barking he called out to Gabby to go see who it was.

Minutes later the child shouted: "Daddy, look!"

In shirt, suit pants, and stocking feet, Oscar went into the living room.

"Grammy looks like a princess!"

Oscar could only stare. Even Mindy had gone quiet, gaping at the new arrivals. Stella was in a satiny, sky-blue ball gown with matching feather boa, and Harold was in a black tuxedo and top hat.

"Are you guys going to the prom?" Oscar said.

Harold was beaming. "You know, we did go to the prom. Nineteen sixty-four. Still had my Elvis Presley haircut."

Stella cracked a smile at the memory, but said nothing.

"Where did you get the clothes?" Oscar said.

"We rented them," Harold said.

"Beauville Bridal," Stella said.

"*Oh, no!*" Harold said.

"What?" Stella said.

"We forgot flowers."

"We don't need flowers," she said. "This is ridiculous enough as it is."

"No, we have to have flowers."

"No we don't."

"At least a corsage. For the pictures," Harold said, his eyes pleading.

Stella shook her head, exasperated.

"I can run over to Stuckey's, on South State," Harold said. "I'll be back in half an hour."

"*No*, you've been running around all morning. Next thing you know, you'll be back at the hospital."

"You know what?" Oscar said. "I'll go."

* * *

At Stuckey's Flower Shop, he chose a pin-on corsage of white ranunculus. A simple arrangement of three flowers on a spray of green leaves. While the woman was wrapping it up, Oscar got a text.

Walter wrote: "You've got to see this. Come by the store if you can." Oscar deleted the text and slid the phone into his trouser pocket.

But back on the bike, heading home, his curiosity caused him to change course. Big Walter's was only a little out of the way. He would swing by and take a quick look.

* * *

It was a mob scene. All up and down West Street, cars, motorcycles, and pickups were driving past Big Walter's, honking their horns, shouting out support, and flying American flags. In front of the store the crowd was dense. There were picket signs and more flags. In addition to the stars and stripes were a few yellow "Don't Tread on Me" flags with coiled rattlesnakes.

Because of all the activity, including a number of cops in the street motioning people along, the traffic was moving slow. As he was about to pass by, Oscar saw Walter, still in his neck brace, waving both arms at him. Oscar pulled the bike over to the side of the road, in front of the store. A cop came and told him to move on but Walter said, "Charlie, he's with me." The cop nodded and went back to directing the flow.

"You made it!" Walter boomed over the din, his face charged, exhilarated.

Oscar killed the engine. "Yeah, I had to run an errand."

The horns kept honking. Someone shouted "Wall-tah!"

Walter waved, beaming. "Hey Barb!"

Scanning the crowd, Oscar was stunned by the turnout. There were a good hundred people, packed into the not-so-large parking lot. Some of them stood, others sat in lawn chairs. Their signs had a range of messages:

"Honk for Freedom!"

"We Are Q"

"End the Bolshevik Media Monopoly"

"Four More Beers!"

"Come And Take It!" (which had the black silhouette of a machine gun)

A handful of guys, with dark sunglasses and grim expressions, wore tan military fatigues and carried semi-automatic weapons. But the overwhelming majority seemed like ordinary citizens, most likely Walter's friends and customers. They were talking and laughing, socializing and having fun. The mood was festive and light, like a street carnival. There were even a couple gas grills going, sending up plumes of smoke and the smell of charring animal flesh.

"This is great, huh?" Walter said.

"Looks like a party," Oscar said. "Apart from the guns."

"Well ... Beano said they're not loaded. It's more about the optics."

"The optics."

"Yeah."

Oscar pondered this. "Walter, are you sure you've thought this through?"

"What do you mean?"

But before Oscar could explain, someone shouted "They're coming!"

Everyone looked to the street. The cops were now redirecting traffic, clearing the road.

"Here we go!" Walter said.

One of the guys in fatigues stepped in front of the crowd. He was holding a bullhorn.

"That's Beano," Walter said.

Through the bullhorn, Beano addressed the throng: "All right everybody, it's time. When they get here, let's drown the commies out!"

All eyes turned to the left. Down the now-empty street, more than a hundred yards away, were the protesters. They were on foot and were being led by a slow-moving police cruiser. Behind the cruiser, Oscar saw a sea of signs and a huge mass of people. Bongo drums, referee whistles, and the chanting of human voices resounded, growing louder as the group approached.

Soon, the front of the pack came into clear view—and Oscar's mouth fell open. Leading the procession, two marchers held aloft a large banner that read,

A Protest Against Hate

Sponsored by Perilloux Motors

Just behind this, in the frontline of marchers, was brother Duncan. He was at the center of a row of ten or so people, men and women, all with their arms interlocked. At Duncan's side was Logan Stoltenham himself, the hero of the hour, and together they seemed to be leading the chant. Although the chorus of voices was becoming ever louder, Oscar couldn't quite make out their words over the general hubbub, which just then got even more raucous as Beano, along with everyone behind Oscar, started their own chant, shouting: "Wall-tah! Wall-tah! Wall-tah!"

Finally, when the protesters had neared to within twenty yards of the store, their words became intelligible. Duncan and the rest of them were saying: "Hey hey! Ho ho! Sexual predators have got to go! Hey hey! Ho ho! Sexual predators have got to go!"

Switching tactics, Beano raised his bullhorn and shouted, "Music!" From unseen speakers came the near-deafening blare of Bruce Springsteen's "Born in the U.S.A." Walter's people went nuts, cheering and waving their signs.

Across the street the slow-moving police cruiser pulled into the park and the marchers began to file in. They had a tremendous crowd, three to four times the size of Walter's. Their demographic was noticeably different as well. Young middle-class parents pushed strollers or walked with their children, whose faces had been painted with rainbows and peace signs. There were also a good amount of graying and white-haired folks echoing the chant with benevolent smiles and intentions. But the great majority of the marchers were angry-faced youngsters, teens and twentysomethings. Blazing with righteous fury, they passed from the street into the park, pumping their fists, raising middle fingers, and shouting obscenities and threats. Among their signs Oscar read:

"Boycott the Bullyboy!"

"Die Fascist Scum"

"Sexual He-rassers Will Pay!"

"Destroy Capitalism!"

"Beauville Savings Bank Promotes Diversity"

A podium had been set up at the edge of the park, near the street, and it was here that Duncan now stood. Oscar had no desire to interact with his brother; it was getting late, and he had a wedding to get to. Yet just as Oscar was about to start up the motorcycle and slip off, Duncan turned to face Big Walter's and the two brothers made eye contact. Feeling caught, feeling trapped, Oscar held up a hand in a resigned wave. Duncan didn't return the wave. Instead, with a look of disgust, he shook his head. Oscar let out a heavy sigh, got off the bike, and crossed the street.

"Look at you," Duncan sneered. "Hanging out with those right-wing crazies. Unbelievable."

"Calm down," Oscar said. "I was just driving by. I had to pick up something for Ma." Then, noticing the Perilloux Motors pin fastened to Duncan's polo jersey, he said, "I see you're living up to your pledge."

"What?"

" 'Making a Better World,' " Oscar read, pointing to the pin.

"Keep laughing, Oscar. And I'll keep laughing to the bank."

"That's pretty cynical."

"No. It's not. It's business. I'm giving the people what they want. Look around … It's democracy in action."

Surveying the scene, Oscar said, "Is that what this is?" On one side of the street there were men with guns, on the other, a wrathful mob clamoring for confrontation, if not violence. To Oscar it was unsettling, and vaguely ominous. And what on earth, he wondered, did any of this have to do with Walter?

"Everything's changing little brother. More than you know," Duncan said. "It's time you got off the fence and got into line. Trust me, you don't want to be on the wrong side. These kids want blood. Anyway, stick around. I'm about to give a speech."

"Sounds like fun. But I have to get back. The wedding's starting soon."

"OK. I should be there around three or four. Tell Margot I'll see her soon."

"I'll do that."

Amid the malicious shouts and insults coming now from both sides, Oscar crossed West Street back to his bike.

Walter came over. "What's Duncan doing?"

"Drumming up business."

Despite the brace constricting his head and torso, Walter shook with laughter.

Oscar said, "You know who I haven't seen, is Pam."

"She's not coming."

"You talked to her?"

"Yeah. The other night I went to the Brewhouse. I wanted to invite her to come today."

"You're kidding."

"No. Hell, why not? After she came to the store and we talked, I thought maybe … you know. But she wasn't interested. She said she wanted nothing to do with either side."

Oscar made no comment. He put on his helmet and got on the bike.

"You heading out?"

"Yeah, I have to go. If you want, stop by my place afterward. Duncan's paying for a caterer and an open bar. The two of you can talk politics. Could be entertaining."

Walter grinned. "Sounds good."

People around them began pointing to the sky. Walter struggled to raise his gaze. Oscar looked up too. A large bird was circling high over the scene.

"It's an eagle," someone said.

"Yeah, it's an eagle," Walter said.

"That's not an eagle," Oscar said. "It's a buzzard."

He kick-started the motorcycle, looked over his shoulder, saw the way was clear, then sped off for home.

NINETEEN

By the time he arrived it was nearly quarter to two. Corsage in hand, Oscar hurried up the stairs and into the living room. Margot's twins were sitting on the sofa.

In unison they said, "Hi Mr. Perilloux!"

"Oh, hello girls. It's great to see you. How've you been?"

"Gooood!" they both said.

He looked at them, wondered which was which, then gave up. "Where's your mother?"

"In the bathroom," one of them said.

"With Gabby," the other one said.

Oscar went to the bathroom. Standing near the sink in just her panties and the new shoes Oscar had recently bought her, Gabby looked crestfallen, her lower lip jutting out. Beside her, Margot was using a face cloth to scrub Gabby's new dress.

From the doorway Oscar said hello—and nearly lost his breath. Each time he saw Margot she was more beautiful than before. It was almost painful.

She returned the greeting, then glanced sadly at Gabby.

"What happened?" Oscar said to the child.

"I spilled Kool-Aid on my dress."

"Oh no."

Gabby nodded, and looked ready to burst into tears.

"I've almost got the stains out," Margot said. "Then we'll dry it with a blow dryer. Everything will be fine," she added, smiling at the child. To Oscar she said, in a hushed voice, "Who hired the DJ?"

"I did. Is he here?"

"Yes. Where did you get him?"

"Craigslist."

Margot raised her eyebrows. "He's been playing acid house for the past twenty minutes."

"Right. I'll go talk to him."

* * *

Entering the kitchen on his way to the backyard, Oscar came upon Stella, Harold, and a woman he didn't know, seated at the table.

"The corsage!" Harold said.

Oscar handed it to him, and Harold, still in his top hat, inspected the arrangement through the clear plastic wrap. "Oh, look at that," he said. "It's beautiful. A beauty for a beauty," he added, looking at Stella.

A glimmer of pleasure came into her eyes, but as always she acted as if she was unmoved. "Remind me not to get married again," she said.

Harold thanked Oscar and asked how much he owed him. Oscar told him to forget it and Harold thanked him again. Then he said, "Oscar, this is Candy Hisslop, justice of the peace."

The woman was older than Oscar, mid-fifties, and had a relaxed, confident demeanor. She remained seated but gave him a
polite smile, saying, "I'm friends with Shirley, Harold's daughter.
We grew up together."

"You know, you look familiar," Oscar said.

"I get that all the time. I sell real estate. You've probably seen
the signs."

"Yes. That's right," Oscar said, now recalling the handful of
for-sale signs he'd seen around Beauville, in people's yards, featuring a color image of Candy Hisslop's relaxed, confident face.

"I also do massage therapy," she said.

"Really," Oscar said.

"Yes. I could give you my card."

Oscar nodded, silently. Then he said, "Just out of curiosity,
what's the ceremony going to be like?"

"Today's ceremony?"

"Yes."

Candy Hisslop's face brightened, and she gave Oscar a look
that seemed meant both to impress and to reassure. "Well, it's
a fairly short service, which is something I find my clients appreciate. First I'll say a few words about Harold and Stella—
that's what we're doing now, I'm getting to know your mom.
Then I'll ask members of the audience to share any memories
or feelings they might have related to the couple or the moment.
This is a chance for people to express themselves and bond with
those around them. I find it's often very moving. Friendships are
formed. Next, I'll recite a poem that I composed myself—a sort
of tribute to love and the human spirit. And finally, I'll read the

'official' parts, the parts supplied by the state, and then I'll ask Harold to kiss the bride." She laughed merrily. "And that's it!"

* * *

Outside, the backyard was completely transformed. The tent was up and the dancefloor laid down. There were cloth-covered tables with chairs under the tent, and nearby were the caterer's buffet setup and bar. Oscar recognized several of the servers from Duncan's Fourth of July cookout.

Four guests had already arrived. Seated together at one of the tables, they were looking with some bewilderment at the DJ, who was just then playing some very loud base-heavy beats. The guy stood at a podium with an opened laptop. He wore bulky headphones and held a hand over one of the ear pieces, bobbing to the music. In addition to the headphones he wore an unbuttoned short-sleeve shirt over a wife-beater tank top, blue-jean shorts that reached down below his knees, and red high-tops. All in all, this wasn't quite what Oscar had expected. The Craigslist ad had read, "DJ for weddings, graduations, and other occasions. Ten years' experience." It had seemed OK.

When Oscar approached him, the guy didn't look up. He was too engrossed with the music and his laptop. Oscar leaned forward and waved a hand.

"Oh, hey," the guy said, over the noise.

"Terry?" Oscar said.

"Uh-huh."

"I'm Oscar. We spoke on the phone the other day."

"Right, cool. How ya been?"

"Good. Would you mind lowering that for a minute?"

The music was lowered.

"Thanks," Oscar said. "So, we're just about ready to start."

"Cool. I'm ready to go."

"OK ... Hey, uh, I did say this was a wedding, right?"

"Oh yeah. Most def."

"Good. Because this doesn't really sound like wedding music to me."

Terry's face went blank.

"And about half of the people coming today are in their seventies," Oscar said, then discreetly nodded in the direction of the folks sitting at the nearby table.

Terry looked over at the four seniors who were quietly watching him, and he still didn't quite seem to get Oscar's point.

"Let me put it another way," Oscar said. "Do you take requests?"

"Oh, yeah. Sure. It's totally cool. It's all done through the computer. I can play whatever you want."

* * *

Soon most of the guests had arrived, and nearly all of them were Harold's people. In a way it seemed appropriate, since this was really his day—the fulfillment of a lifelong dream. There were his children and their families, his two siblings and their families, his bowling team and his VFW buddies and their wives. Stella, alas, had no friends, and so that left only her children. And of those, only Oscar was now present.

Everyone was gathered under the big tent, mingling at tables or on the dancefloor, holding drinks and chatting and laughing as Frank Sinatra played in the background. It was a beautiful August day, sunny but not humid. Perfect for a wedding. After a stressful morning, Oscar was ready to relax and enjoy himself. Stella had her corsage, the DJ had a new playlist, and Gabby's dress had been restored almost to new. The child was giddily running around with Zora and Sana, the three of them already acting like the best of friends. Margot, radiant with good-feeling, was circulating just as she had done at Duncan's cookout, effortlessly engaging people and putting them at their ease. Oscar, less socially adept than she, nonetheless managed to follow her lead, and found it a delight to mix with all the new faces.

* * *

With Candy Hisslop presiding, the ceremony went off according to plan. Many people seemed to enjoy it. There was good-natured laughter at some of the shared Harold-and-Stella memories; a few shed tears as Candy read her sentimental poem; and a great cheer from all when Harold finally kissed the bride. For the meal, Oscar, Margot, and the girls shared a table. Oscar and Margot both went with the Lazy Man's Lobster. The twins went with the cheeseburger. And Gabby went with the sole vegetarian option, something called "Faux Chicken Piccata." According to the child, it was "really yummy."

While they ate Oscar got two texts. The first was from Walter: "All hell broke loose. Those punk millennials started a riot and tried to trash my store. Not sure I can make the wedding." The second was from Duncan: "Don't think I can make the wedding. Walter's militia buddies started a riot. I took a billy club to the head and am now at the hospital getting stitches. Meeting with the press afterward. Fantastic day. Tell Margot I'll call her." Oscar deleted both messages. After the second one, Margot said, "What's going on?"

"It's Duncan. He won't be coming."

Margot said nothing, though her reaction made it clear she wasn't too upset. Neither was Oscar. Everything seemed fine as it was. In fact, things couldn't have been better. Harold and Stella seemed happy, all the guests seemed happy, the three girls seemed happy, and Margot seemed happy. As for Oscar, he was beyond happy. It was just one of those days.

* * *

After the meal came the cake, and after the cake came the first dance. As the happy couple walked onto the dancefloor, with Harold gallantly towing Stella's air tank, the guests began to clap.

Over the PA, Terry the DJ said: "Yo yo yo! Let's hear it for the newlyweds!"

The clapping grew louder, and some of the VFW guys called out to their friend:

"All right Harold!"

"Yay Harold-boy!"

"Go get 'em big fella!"

At the center of the dancefloor, Stella removed the air hose from her nostrils and set it on the tank. Harold removed his top hat and handed it to Terry. Then, from the speakers, there came the gentle strumming of an acoustic guitar, followed by the heartfelt voice of Elvis Presley—the opening to "Love Me Tender." As the King crooned for his eternal love, Harold took Stella into his arms. Very gently, very tenderly, he embraced his own eternal love and led her in a slow, slow dance.

Oscar's eyes were stinging, the tears welling. Gabby, entranced by all that was happening, paused to look at her dad.

"What's wrong?" she said.

"A bug," he said. "Flew in my eye."

The child turned back to the action. But then Oscar noticed Margot: she was watching him. He felt a flutter of embarrassment, didn't want her to see him like this. He refocused on the dance.

When the song ended the applause was boisterous. There were whistles and shouts.

Terry the DJ said, "At this time Harold and Stella would invite everyone onto the dancefloor." Over the speakers came the opening notes to "Islands in the Stream"—Kenny Rogers and Dolly Parton.

"Oh, I love this song!" Margot said, looking at Oscar.

The words, and especially her eager eyes, sent a thrill through his body, an electric buzz. Drunk with emotion, and also a little drunk from the booze, Oscar rose to his feet. Like some gentleman of old, he extended his hand and led Margot out onto the floor.

The song is mid-tempo, and while some couples stood apart, dancing freestyle, others opted for a more intimate embrace. Oscar left the decision to Margot. Lady's choice. Eyes gleaming with joy, her smile warm and bright, she held open her arms, inviting him close. He stepped forward and placed his hands around her waist. And meeting her gaze with his own, Oscar thought, Thank you. Thank you.

About the Author

Michael Lacoy is the author of *The Mystical Adventures of Stavros Papadakis*. He lives in New Hampshire.

CPSIA information can be obtained
at www.ICGtesting.com
Printed in the USA
LVHW030230070421
683674LV00009B/509

9 780960 068937